Glass Cutter
A Sgt Major Crane crime thriller

Wendy Cartmell

Copyright © Wendy Cartmell 2015
Published by Costa Press
ISBN-13: 978-1511519359
ISBN-10: 1511519355
Wendy Cartmell has asserted her right under the Copyright Designs and Patents Act 1998 to be identified as the author of this work.
All characters and events in this publication, other than those in the public domain, are fictitious and any resemblance to real persons, living or dead is purely coincidental
This is a work of fiction and not meant to represent faithfully military, or police, policies and procedures. All and any mistakes in this regard are my own.
Inspired by a friend and fellow writer.

Praise for Wendy Cartmell
'A pretty extraordinary talent' –
Best Selling Crime Thrillers
'This is genre fiction at its best, suspense that rivets and a mystery that keeps you guessing.' –
A R Symmonds on Goodreads.

Also by Wendy Cartmell

Sgt Major Crane books:
Steps to Heaven
40 Days 40 Nights
Honour Bound
Cordon of Lies
Regenerate
Hijack
Glass Cutter
Solid Proof

Crane and Anderson crime thrillers
Death Rites
Death Elements
Death Call
A Grave Death

Emma Harrison Mysteries
Past Judgement
Mortal Judgement
Joint Judgement

One

Louise Marshall passed the back of her hand across her brow. She'd been unpacking all morning and looked at the mass of boxes littering the sitting room of their new army quarter. Well, not so much new, as old, she supposed. The house was imposing, as befitting a commanding officer, a solid Victorian house, set in large gardens. The resultant quietness was calming, but if she were honest, a little isolating. No longer could she hear the chatter of women, clattering of children's feet, or cars being backed off drives. Now she only heard bird song, or the occasional mewling of cats.

There was a whole world outside the gates, which were as large and imposing as the drive they protected. But somehow the house made her not want to go out there. Out there was new. A new garrison, new wives, new subordinates. For as the Colonel's wife, or as the army would put it, the wife of Colonel Marshall, Royal Logistics Corp, Travers Barracks, Aldershot, she was expected to get involved. Her duties would include meeting her husband's subordinates, greeting them by name, asking after their wives and their children. She rather needed a notebook, she realised. She'd never remember everyone's names and writing them down would help her memorise them. She must remember to ask Peter that evening to run through the people she needed to recall. When he came home. If he came home.

Shaking such thoughts away she turned her mind back to the job in hand and began to stack the empty boxes, placing smaller ones inside larger ones, until she had a pile in the hallway. She looked up at the imposing stairway and around the elegant hall of their new home. The overall impression was of high ceilings and deep mahogany wood that gleamed. She imagined the shine was because of the countless servants that had diligently polished it over the years. Through an open door at the back of the house she could see into the large kitchen that was, luckily, not as old as the house. It had been dragged into the twentieth century and sported all the modern appliances and was where she would be expected to produce wonderful dinners. They would be for men who were far more interested in drinking and wives who were more interested in taking stock of her than eating her cuisine. Louise could feel their eyes on her already.

They would wonder if she looked young for her age, or old. Did she dress right and sound right? Was she friendly or slightly frosty? Did she peer down at everyone from her elevated position as the Colonel's wife, or would she muck in and get her hands dirty?

Turning her gaze away from the kitchen, Louise looked at herself in the lovely old gilt framed mirror that had been hanging on the wall when they arrived. It was so large and imposing, there wasn't really anywhere else to put it, so she had decided to leave it hanging there. It was handy to use to check her appearance when they left for whatever function or duty was to be performed that day or night. Today she looked pale, she decided, inspecting her skin tone in the antique glass. She really should put some make up on and brush out her auburn hair which was breaking free from the twisted knot she'd hastily pinned up that morning. Her cat-like green eyes would benefit from a sweep of mascara and her chapped lips from some lipstick. Peter had always instilled in her that you never knew if anyone would call unexpectedly and he would expect her to be ready for anything and everything. He expected her to be the perfect army wife.

And thinking of which, it was about time she got rid of these boxes. Under the stairs, set into the wooden panelling that graced the wall under the banister, was a small door. Peter had said it led to the cellar, somewhere where she had yet to explore. The perfect place to store boxes, she decided, where they'd be out of sight, out of mind.

She really should go out and do some food shopping, she thought, as she glanced at her watch, yet she was hesitant to leave the house. Somehow it felt safer here, tucked away from the hustle and bustle of the garrison, away from the watching, prying eyes that would be monitoring her every move. So instead of walking up the stairs to put on a face for the world and change out of her jeans and tee-shirt, she walked towards the door to the basement. She'd stay a while and explore the house, she thought, as her hand reached for the door handle.

The stairs surprised her, being concrete; somehow she'd expected rickety wooden ones, leading down to a cellar full of cobwebs, spiders and the odd dead mouse. She stood at the top, grasping for a light. As her hand felt a plastic plate, she flicked the switch on and took a few hesitant steps downward. A strip light struggled, flicking on and off, before settling down and buzzing into life, illuminating the cellar with its harsh light.

She leaned over the banister and saw that the area was large, seemingly running underneath most of the house. It was split into sections. There was a work bench, stained and marked from unknown tools and metal shelves that were ready to hold Peter's bits and bobs, the solitary oil can waiting patiently for other tins to join it. Louise walked down the remaining steps and past the workbench and shelves. She came to a large boiler, clanking and working overtime to keep the house above warm. Moving further into the cellar, she could see the back wall was roughly plastered, as though the workman had become overwhelmed by the size of the job he had taken on. As the far corner of the cellar was not on view, it seemed he hadn't bothered to produce his best work there.

Turning back towards the stairs, Louise saw something pushed up against the side wall of the cellar. Walking over to it, she saw it was an old travelling chest, of the type used many years before by boys going off to boarding school, or soldiers travelling to their next posting. Kneeling down, she ran her hands over the old cracked leather, brittle beneath her fingers. There was a label tied to it and looking closely at the old fashioned writing in black ink against the yellowing paper, she read the name Underwood. Man or boy? She had no idea.

The natural thing to do would be to open the chest and peer inside. But Louise hesitated. Looking behind her she made sure no one was watching. A stupid gesture as she was alone in the house. But she'd had the feeling, for a fleeting moment, that she wasn't on her own. It was probably just a change in temperature as the boiler has just fired up, she reasoned. But still, opening the chest felt like an invasion of someone's privacy. A nonsensical notion, as it was more than likely empty, Louise thought. So she took a breath and lifted the lid.

Secretly hoping it to be full of treasures, such as old clothes, shoes, boots and pictures, she was disappointed to find only one item in there. It appeared to be a scarf of some kind as Louise could see white silk. Reaching for it, she realised it was covering something. Something hard. A book perhaps? A diary?

Using both hands, she lifted it out of the chest, rocking back on her heels. The silk headscarf shimmered as it slithered away, revealing what appeared to be a large scrap book, or maybe a photo album. The light at the back of the cellar wasn't very bright, so Louise put the scarf back in the chest and took the book over to the concrete steps. Sitting on the first one, she placed the book on her knees. She could now see that the large red leather book had something written on the cover. There were just two words embossed on the leather, Matilda Underwood. Intrigued, Louise opened the book…

Two

My name is Matilda Underwood and this is my story. It's not a new one. It's the story of every other disaffected, displaced and abused individual. What makes my story different is how I dealt with it. How I dealt with the rejection, the misunderstanding, the mistreatment.

I came to this house hoping for redemption. And in a way I got it, I suppose. Just not in the way I imagined. But more of that later.

On first sight I loved this house. It wrapped its arms around me like the mother I had never known. It made me feel wanted, loved, secure. In fact it is the only thing in my life that ever has. A house, after all, is solid and safe. Not like human beings. They are fickle, flawed, cruel and unusual. My past experiences mean that I no longer trust people. Men, women, children, it makes no difference. They have all hurt me in one way or another. At one time or another. But not this house. There was always a nook or a cranny revealed to me, that I could hide myself in, when the pressures of the life I lead and had led, got too much.

One of my hiding places was the attic. I loved poking around in there, trying on old clothes, slipping them on like a new persona; sitting in discarded furniture; setting out ornaments; playing the lady of the manor. I was as happy as a child given dolls and a tea set to play with. Most days I could be found either there or in the cellar. Underneath the house lay tools that I'd never seen before. Implements that I shuddered to think what they could be used for. Half used tins of paint and pots of foul smelling liquid. All fascinating in their own way. I would make up uses for them, imagine them being used by old gnarled hands, lovingly cleaned and cared for. Relics of the past, memories of a time long gone by. A happier time? Who knows. But perhaps a simpler time.

I found this old book one day in the attic and rescued it. I was sorting through some old discarded newspapers and as I revealed it, the red leather cover beckoned me. I ran my hands over the hide and it warmed them, the book seeming to speak to me. Its pages were blank and I had the uncanny feeling that they were eager to be filled with a story that was just waiting to be told.

I carried the book carefully down the narrow steep attic stairs and took it to my room. There I cleaned and polished the cover, brushed the cobwebs off it and separated some stuck pages. When I'd finished, it sat on my dressing table waiting. But it wasn't quite ready to be used.

The next day I took it into town to a local printer. I was unsure if he could help, but he assured me he could. And this is the result. My name embossed in gold on the cover. Isn't it beautiful?

Now the book is ready and so am I. It's time I told my tale.

Three

Before she could turn the next page, Louise was startled by a noise from up above. It was Peter. She didn't know why she was so surprised, for who else could it have been? No one else would walk into the house unannounced. No one would dare. As Peter called her, driven by some instinct she couldn't put a name to, Louise quickly returned the book to the chest, determined not to mention her find.

Thinking back on why she did that, she decided that perhaps it was nothing more than wanting something that belonged to her alone. For after all her life wasn't her own, it was dictated by her husband and her husband's life was dictated by the army. The more she thought about it, the more she resolved that she wouldn't share Matilda's book. It would be her secret.

For the rest of the day they worked together on the house. Peter piled the empty boxes in the cellar for her and then went outside and spent the rest of the afternoon sorting through the garage, occasionally bringing through things to store in the basement. She unpacked the rest of the kitchen equipment, crockery and cutlery. She arranged pots and pans near the stove, put the china further away from it and nominated cupboards for foodstuff. Then moving through to the sitting room she pushed and pulled chairs and sofas this way and that until they were arranged to her liking. She plumped cushions, dusted off lamps and scattered rugs.

By the end of the day, Louise was too exhausted to do much more for dinner than heat some leftover casserole and put a baguette in the oven to warm. They ate their food on trays balanced on their knees in front of the television.

Louise watched Peter eating. He always ate quickly, as though needing to get the meal out of the way and move on to other more interesting things. A throwback from being on exercise or in theatre, she supposed, where food was nothing more than a necessity. Fuel. Not something to be slowly enjoyed, relishing every mouthful. He tossed back his wine as though it were lager and put the empty glass back on his tray. He was fresh out of the shower and beads of water glistened in his short dark hair. He wore a simple white tee-shirt that clung to his slim frame and baggy joggers that hid his muscular thighs and calves.

Not much interested in the news and feeling the need to make conversation she asked Peter how things were going at the barracks.

'Fine. Why?' he answered his eyes still on the television.

'I just wondered. Do you think you'll like it here?'

'Of course,' he looked at her in surprise. 'Why on earth wouldn't I?'

Why wouldn't he indeed, she realised. For Peter things were the same on every barracks in every garrison. The same tasks, routines, policies and procedures. The army structure was the same the world over. Things only seemed changed for her. She was the one who seemed to find it all so unnerving. She quaked at the thought of the new house, new people and new responsibilities, every time he climbed yet another rung on the ladder of promotion. Every time they moved she was at sea. While he? He took it all in his stride.

Later in bed, she turned to him, slipped her arms around his waist and kissed his neck. It wasn't that he didn't love her. Wasn't that he mistreated her. He just, well, didn't seem to take much notice of her. She wondered if tonight would be any different. Could she make him see her? Make him feel her love? Make him feel her need? She caressed his back, felt the broad shoulders and well defined muscles under her fingertips. If the light had been on, she would have been able to see the scars that tattooed his body. One from where he was shot. Another from a skiing accident. A third from an operation.

'Peter?' she whispered in the dark, unable to hide the hope in her voice.

'Not tonight, eh, darling. Busy day tomorrow,' he said and burrowed further under the duvet.

He moved away from her. Only slightly. But enough to cause her hand to fall off his back and land in the space between them.

A casual rejection, yet the pain of it sliced her in two. Why was he indifferent to her, she wondered. Unmoved by her advances. So dismissive of her love. Louise listened to the rhythmic ticking of the grandfather clock they had placed in the hallway and that could be heard through the open bedroom door. Its rhythmic tick tock, tick tock, sounded loud in the otherwise silent house. Eventually it lulled her to sleep.

1976

Father Chumley, Arch Deacon of all he surveyed, was sitting behind his desk in his study. It was a typically male space, he supposed, looking around it. Winged armchairs, large desk, angle poise lamp placed just so, to illuminate the godly words he was writing and that he would preach to his congregation on Sunday. It was Harvest Festival. He'd preached the same sermon now for the past five years so he'd thought he'd have a go at writing something different for this year. Although he wasn't altogether sure that people remembered what he'd said from one Sunday to the next, never mind from one year to the next. He sighed. Oh well, as he was now Arch Deacon, a most prized appointment, a bit like being an area manager, he really felt he ought to raise his game. You never knew when someone higher up the ecclesiastical chain would slip into the back of the church anonymously, intent on doing an unannounced spot check. Spies sent by the Bishop.

He realised he was wool gathering, wasting time, so he picked up his pen and once more bent over his words. He'd only written five sentences and had an awfully long way to go yet. He was just composing a particularly brilliant phrase when the telephone rang. He sighed as the words flew out of his brain and instead of being put down on the paper, they vanished into thin air. He put down his pen and picked up the receiver, anything to stop the incessant, shrill bell.

By the time he got rid of the Chairwoman of the Women's Institute, who had some silly questions about the Harvest Supper, he had no idea what he had been writing about, so had to read his five sentences all over again. He'd just got to the end when he heard the mail plop through the letterbox and onto the hall carpet. He pushed away his chair and hurried into the hall to get his letters before his housekeeper reached them first. Otherwise she'd flick through each one, telling him who they were from and asking annoying questions. Not prying exactly, more wanting to keep up to date with goings on in the vicarage. At least that's what she would say by way of explanation.

He placed the unopened letters on the edge of his desk and bent to his sermon. But he kept seeing the post out of the corner of his eye. Kept wondering who the letters were from and what they were about. Realising he wouldn't get another word written until he knew the contents of the correspondence, he once more put down his pen and grabbed them eagerly with one hand while reaching for his letter opener with another.

But after all that they were a little disappointing, an electricity bill, which the parish paid for, a reminder that his car needed a service and a request for a christening. For good measure Mr Soames had sent him a note asking if he wanted to be part of a Football Pools syndicate. Didn't Soames realise he was a member of God's syndicate? He couldn't be seen to be gambling.

Sighing in frustration at the idiocy of some of his congregation, he once more picked up his pen, determined to write his sermon. He was just mouthing the next few words, when there was a knock at his study door. Before he could speak it was flung open and in walked his housekeeper, Mrs Hardy. At this third interruption he nearly threw his pen at her, but caught himself just in time. He couldn't have her gossiping about him throughout the Parish, telling people of his indiscretions, so he tightened his grip on the pen and forced a smile onto his lips.

'Yes, Mrs Hardy? What is it?' He couldn't help snapping a little, his tone conveying his exasperation.

'Just brought your coffee, Father. It's just how you like it, made with hot milk.' The cup rattled in the saucer as she carried it across the room. She hadn't seemed to notice his brusque tone, she was probably used to it after many years of looking after him. She continued speaking, 'I've put a couple of fig biscuits on the side. I know how much you like them.'

In fact Father Chumley had rather gone off them since she'd started giving them to him morning, noon and night. He'd tried to tell her that he fancied a change, but she hadn't yet taken the hint.

'Thank you, Mrs Hardy,' he said, as she placed the milky brew on his desk, hoping she'd leave straightaway. But she didn't. She started chatting aimlessly about her excursion to the market that morning.

'And because I went early,' she said to him, 'I managed to get some really good fresh vegetables for your dinner this evening. Then, I was just looking through some aprons, for in truth the one I have is becoming rather threadbare and it has a few stains on it that I just can't seem to get out,' she paused and scratched away at a part of her apron, before recovering herself. 'Anyway, sorry, got a bit side tracked there for a moment. What I wanted to say was that you'll never guess who I saw across the way in the market. I saw her but I don't think she saw me.'

Father Chumley looked suitably perplexed.

'It was that girl you used to help,' Mrs Hardy said. 'It was quite a few years ago now, I suppose. Doesn't time fly? Anyway as I was saying, I'm sure it was her. Same ginger hair and green eyes. What was her name? It's on the tip of my tongue... oh yes, Matilda, that's it. That lovely girl Matilda, you know the one who you counselled for ages. You tried to help her, the poor orphan. She looks stunning now, mind you, if it was her that is. What's the matter, Father?'

Father Chumley had managed to stop her flood of words by coughing, very loudly, several times.

'Oh, yes, sorry, Father, I'd best let you get on,' she took the hint and much to his relief turned away from his desk and walked out of the study, closing the door behind her.

To begin with, as Mrs Hardy had been talking, Father Chumley thought that someone had opened a window, allowing freezing cold air to pour across his neck and shoulders. It enveloped his back like dry ice, sending shivers down it. Shivers that were equally frightening and equally thrilling. For Matilda had been the most delicious young girl and it seems she was still as striking now as she had been back then. It had been a privilege to have her, to mould her, to make her his own. But of course, if the truth be told, the privilege had been all hers. He had chosen her over many other girls in the orphanage. She'd been blessed by his attention, by the hours she'd spent in his company.

But then the dread set in, that cold shiver of concern. She had always been a bit headstrong, his Matilda, more difficult to break than the others. He wondered what she was doing in the area. Thought how strange it was that she should be shopping in the market just a few hundred yards from his house. He wondered if she was looking for him, but why would she be? Could she....? No, not possibly. She couldn't be here to hurt him. To pay him back for the things he'd done when she was young, surely not. She must miss him. Yes, that would be it, Father Chumley decided. Yearn for him. Need to be with him. For hadn't he looked after her so diligently?

And so he squashed his dread, unable to entertain the possibility that Matilda could want to harm him. For why should she? He had loved her so.

Four

Peter left the house the next morning, forgetting to kiss Louise goodbye, intent as he was on returning to his beloved barracks. But for once it didn't seem to matter as much as it normally did. For today Louise had something she needed to do for once. As soon as Peter was out of the house, she clattered down the basement steps to retrieve the book from the chest. A flutter of excitement brewed within her, something she'd not felt for a very long time. For any excitement she'd once felt about Peter being in the army, had morphed into dread somewhere along the years. What people had failed to realise, namely her family and her husband, was that she was a particularly solitary person, shy and introspective. She wasn't sure if it was in her nature, or just the way her nomadic childhood had moulded her. So all the new this and new that terrified her more than it would a 'normal' army wife. At times she felt as though she should walk a few steps behind Peter, not out of some religious respect, but so that he could shield her from people. Shield her from life.

As she opened the lid of the chest and unwrapped the book from the silk scarf, a shaft of light fell on the red cover, from a small window set high in the wall. Louise fancied the gold lettering was glowing, welcoming her back. She grabbed the book from the chest and held it close, relieved that it was still safe. Already it was beginning to feel like an old friend.

All yesterday afternoon she'd tensed every time Peter had gone into the cellar, worried in case he found the book. He couldn't, he simply couldn't. If he had, she was afraid he would have tossed it away, seeing it as just another piece of rubbish to be thrown out in his constant quest to clean up his life. And if that had happened she knew she wouldn't have put up a fight. She would have just meekly agreed with him and then secretly retrieved it later on.

She sat down on the concrete steps, but the temperature in the cellar left a lot to be desired and goose bumps were forming on her bare arms. It was too cold to read in the cellar and too uncomfortable, so she tucked the book under her arm and climbed the stairs.

To draw out the anticipation of reading the next entry from Matilda, Louise went into the kitchen. Placing the book carefully on the kitchen table, she cleared away the breakfast things and stacked the dishwasher, all the while her eyes flitting back to the book. When she could take the expectation no longer, she poured herself a cup of coffee and grabbed it off the table. Walking into the sitting room, she curled up in a floral armchair, placed her china cup on a small wooden table nearby and read on……..

Five

It took some searching, but eventually I found the first person who had mistreated me all those years ago, the one that had started this whole chain of events. He'd moved away but the organisation he represented was very helpful and as a result I managed to track his movements around the country. He'd stayed a few months here, a few years there. And then, by a stroke of fate, yes fate not luck, for I truly believed it was meant to be, I found out he'd moved back to this area. Near to the place where it had all started. Not knowing that he had come full circle. Not knowing that his beginning would turn out to be his end.

I drove to his house, trying my best to contain my excitement, for there was no place within me for emotion that night. I knew I must be as cold and calculating as my victim was. I could look forward to enjoying the fruits of my labour afterwards.

My plan was to wait until late at night. Wait until I was confident he was alone. I would then be his last ever visitor. As darkness fell, from across the street, I watched his housekeeper leave, buttoning up her coat against the chill night air as she hurried home. I wondered if she knew what he was on the inside, knew his secret. Surely she mustn't. For how could she continue to work for him if she did? Or at least that was what I hoped.

Then several people arrived. It appeared they were there for a meeting. They came in dribs and drabs and gathered in the lounge, sitting on an assortment of chairs, sofas and even a piano stool. I could see them talking, laughing and making notes through the open curtains. I watched them drink tea and coffee. A few looked like they'd welcome something stronger, but they didn't seem to be offered it. Did the motley crew realise they were being observed? Did they have any inkling that the whole street could see them? They were displayed as brightly as any television screen for my amusement as I sat watching them. But really my eyes were only on him. They locked onto their target like a heat seeking missile and would not be deflected. This time the tables would be turned. This time he was mine. I would be his victim no longer.

It was two hours before they left, by which time I was beyond cold, not wanting to turn the engine on in the car in case it drew attention to my vigil. Luckily I'd worn warm clothes and also brought an old travelling rug I'd found in the attic of the house. The flask of coffee I'd packed had been most welcome, but by then it was empty. I would have to wait until it was time to get out of the car to bring any feeling back to my hands and feet.

I continued to watch his visitors as they passed around coats, hats, gloves and scarves. They struggled into their winter garments, girding their loins, ready for the cold night air. They called to one another and waved goodbye as they left the house and walked away, their breath pluming out and then dissolving in the cold night air. Their words disappeared into the ether, empty platitudes that held no substance. They climbed into cars and with engines roaring and exhausts trembling, their vehicles pulled away. The sound of their engines faded into the distance, until they could be heard no more and the street returned to its previously quiet state.

And still I waited.

I watched him through his window as he did a bit of desultory tidying up after their departure, no doubt preferring to leave the chore for the housekeeper in the morning. My eyes followed him into the next room, the kitchen, where he began to make what appeared to be a mug of coco. He fussed over the milk, making sure he had exactly the right quantity in the pan. He carefully spooned in three level teaspoons of coco powder, scraping the top of each one with a knife. Then he set the pan on the stove. Maybe he had trouble sleeping and needed the soothing brew to help him relax. I laughed mirthlessly to myself. If anyone should be an insomniac it should be him. After what he did to me and goodness knows how many other innocent girls, how could he possibly sleep at night? Maybe he replayed the memories of what he had done to us as his head lay on his pillow. We were the ones who kept him company, warmed his empty bed and made him smile. Took him by the hand and led him to the land of dreams.

I climbed out of my car and after stamping my feet to get some feeling back into them, walked up to his house. I knocked on his door. The bang of the knocker reverberated through the wood, the hollow sound echoing through the house. I experienced no nerves, no qualms about what I was about to do. I knew I was morally justified. He was an evil man who needed to be wiped off the face of the earth.

He opened the door confidently, appearing to not be afraid of whoever it was calling. I supposed he would be used to people arriving late at night, in his line of work, people who required his services, for an ill or infirmed relative who was about to take their final breath. He looked at me, framed in his open door. I stood there, staring back at him. Not speaking. After the initial shock, as my face was dragged up from the annals of his memory, he invited me in, the pleasure of my unexpected visit evident in his reptilian face.

'Oh my,' he said. 'Matilda. Is it really you? Tilly? Come in, come in.' His tongue flicked in and out of his mouth to lick his lips. His already protruding eyes bulged. He must have assumed I had missed his sexual advances and come back for more, as that's where the social niceties ended. But let's face it he never was much of a conversationalist, at least not with me.

Closing the door behind us, he immediately turned and lurched for me, arms outstretched, eyes gleaming. No doubt he was hoping I was as eager as he. He must have been seeing in his mind's eye how I had looked when I was many years younger. But I was no longer a young girl and I was ready for him. As he bore down on me, I brought my knee up to collide with his groin. The pain must have enraged him, for instead of collapsing to the ground so I could break his skull with the rock in my pocket, as I'd anticipated, he grabbed my hair and smashed my face into a mirror hanging on the hall wall. Then he seemed to take great delight in grinding my cheek into the glass, cutting my face to ribbons. That nonchalant cruel act scarred me for life on the outside, as he had already scarred me for life on the inside.

When he eventually let go of my hair, having grown tired of the sport, I stooped down, picked up a shard of glass from the broken mirror that had fallen to the floor and plunged it into his eye. Not stopping until it was driven all the way into his brain. The shock on his face was the most pleasing thing I had ever seen. As his mind closed down and ceased to function, so did his body, crumpling in a heap at my feet. I stepped over his lifeless corpse and left the vicarage. Head held high, triumphant. Father Chumley, the priest who had been the first person to abuse me, could hurt me no more.

Six

Louise closed the book, shocked by what she'd just read. How easily killing had seemed to come to Matilda. Louise thought about killing someone, committing murder. She turned the thought this way and that in her mind. Felt the taste as she mouthed the words written in the book. She read again about the unspeakable act. Then pondered some more. Who could blame Matilda, she decided. Who could stand in judgement of her? It appeared that the vicar had sexually abused Matilda. He had been a paedophile, one of that ugly breed of men who were more and more being exposed. Public figures, celebrities, men who should have lived up to the trust placed in them by their young fans, were being unmasked for the beasts they were. It was always on the news, the list growing daily. Their disgusting ways had been brought to light, even though the events had happened 20, 30, or even 40 years ago. The time frame no longer mattered. No matter how long ago their transgressions, they were being made to pay for their atrocities.

But shining a spotlight on such acts probably wasn't the case in Matilda's time, Louise reasoned. She knew from the recent trials, that in the 1960's and 1970's sexual outrages against minors was just something that happened. Vulnerable victims were from children's homes, orphanages or even those lying ill in bed in hospital. Everyone seemed to know about it, but no one did anything to stop it. There seemed to have been little thought for the victims. People had just shrugged and accepted that it was just the way things were.

The ringing of her mobile phone interrupted Louise's thoughts of Matilda and she picked it up from where it lay next to her now empty coffee cup. She saw skin had formed on the dribble left in the bottom of the delicate, floral painted, china cup. She must have been reading and then lost in thought for some time.

'Hello, darling,' Peter's sugar smooth voice said. 'I just wanted to let you know that I'll be home late tonight.'

'Oh,' Louise said and although she knew that she shouldn't question him, she couldn't help asking, 'Why?'

'Just something on at the Officers' Mess,' he replied casually.

'You never mentioned it before,' Louise pressed him. She wanted to prod him, so he would realise how his absence that evening would make her feel. But she only succeeded in needling him.

'No,' he replied, the silky tone gone now. 'It must have slipped my mind.'

Louise focused on the red velvet curtains they'd hung a few days ago. A warm colour that should have injected atmosphere into the room, but at that moment all Louise could do was shiver at the coldness behind Peter's words. The room was no longer restful and comforting but cold and empty. She knew that nothing ever slipped his mind. He was a bloody soldier. They didn't do slipped minds. Especially not soldiers of his rank. You didn't get to the rank of Colonel by forgetting things.

'This one's not for wives, then?' Her tone was light. But she'd pushed him too far.

'Don't wait up,' he said and cut the call.

In an instant he was gone, the call having lasted less than a minute. There had been no thought as to how she was. No wanting to know what she was doing with her day. He hadn't asked if she was she happy, sad, lonely. She thought that Peter was probably the most selfish man she had ever met.

A tear ran down her face and threatened to drop onto the cover of Matilda's book. Not wanting it to be marked, she wiped the tear away with a tissue grabbed from under the sleeve of her cardigan. Intending to carry on with the unpacking that morning she had picked out a pair of jeans and teamed them with a matching jumper and cardigan for warmth, for the house was chilly. They'd realised the boiler needed servicing as it just wasn't coping with the number of radiators in the house as some were red hot and others lukewarm and they were still waiting for a heating engineer to call.

Replacing her mobile on the table she picked up her cup and saucer and went to the kitchen to get another coffee. As she walked over to the percolator, she saw the pile of ironing waiting to be tackled. As she opened the fridge she saw the food she needed to cook off before it went bad. A smile played across her lips. Sod the chores, the sweeping and cleaning, she decided. Sod the remainder of the unpacking. For once she would do what she wanted to do. Just as Peter always did what he wanted to do, when he wanted to do it.

She might not have her husband with her to keep her company, but she had her friend Matilda. A woman who was as eager to continue telling her story, as Louise was to read it...

Seven

I arrived back at the house, a handkerchief pressed up against my cheek. The once white linen now stained red. As I stumbled in, I said something to my husband about being mugged and being sent sprawling to the floor amongst some broken bottles. I tried to look suitably shocked and upset, which I was, at least as far as my injury went. But I had to be careful to hide the shine of victory in my eyes. The satisfaction I felt about what I had done to the vicar, more than made up for any outward disfigurement I might be left with. At least had I thought that at the time, not knowing that later I would change my mind.

I was immediately taken to the hospital, my husband driving while I sat in the passenger seat. By now I was holding a tea towel to my face, for there was too much blood still seeping through the cuts than a handkerchief could cope with. The doctors looked horrified when they first laid eyes on my previously unblemished face. But then their professionalism kicked in and they hid their initial reaction behind whatever door in their mind they kept locked and bolted. The one that held images of the worst wounds they had seen.

I became cross when they wouldn't let me have a mirror, when they wouldn't let me see my own injuries. Everyone else could look, but not I. I began to feel like an exhibit in a zoo as nurses and doctors paraded in, looking at my cheek, peering this way and that and then leaving without a word, or without actually doing anything to help my injury. The rumour must have gone out - go and see that poor woman's face - and they'd all complied, following each other into my room like lemmings over a cliff.

The plastic surgeon operated on me the next day. For it was best I should be asleep while they pulled out the glass that had become embedded in my flesh, they said. Some of the pieces went so deep they were lodged in my cheekbone apparently. The plastic surgeon said he would do his best invisible stitching, but asked me not to hold out too much hope that I wouldn't be scarred.

It was some weeks before they let me view the damage. They said I needed to be strong enough to cope with the sight of it, both mentally and physically. I had already had a terrible shock from the attack and they seemed concerned that another one might make me lose my mind.

But during that time of waiting and healing I had my secret to keep me company. I began to hear snippets of gossip about the aftermath of my action. Apparently the housekeeper had found the vicar's body the next morning, stumbling over the lifeless form that had lain in the hall since the previous night. She'd screamed bloody murder before fainting and had had to be revived with smelling salts. The local newspaper made much of his passing, writing about how he had spent his life in God's service, working tirelessly for his parishioners and that he would be sadly missed by the faithful.

I alone knew that he would not be sadly missed by a great number of young girls. They might cry when they read the newspaper reports. But they would shed tears of gladness, not sadness. Father Chumley might not have been brought to justice, been made to answer for his crime, but instead he had died for them. Some might think that his death was a better option than him being locked up in prison for years. Capital punishment was no longer on the statute books, having been abolished in 1965, so *the state would have had to look after him until he died. I supposed that one way of looking at it was that I had saved them the expense.*

The police investigation didn't seem to be going anywhere. They had no witnesses, no finger prints, just an approximate time of death, sometime late evening to early morning. I was thrilled by their inability to find any clues. It looked as though I was going to get away with it.

When the doctors eventually let me look in the mirror, I saw my cheek was a mass of scar tissue. It was as though I had a road map printed on the side of my face, complete with bumps and lumps signifying hills and holes and depressions for valleys. The roads went here and there, everywhere and nowhere. Everyone was very kind. But I could see the pity in their eyes.

Perhaps this was to be my punishment for killing someone, for taking another's life. For committing cold blooded murder. The police couldn't find me, but I knew what I'd done. I'd weighed up if taking his life was just punishment for ruining mine and many, many others and I'd found him guilty as charged.

It seemed my face was healed. But my mind was not. I became a recluse for a while. The hospital offered me an appointment with a psychiatrist, but I decided that no amount of talking could change the way I now looked. Anyway I didn't want anyone delving into my mind for who knew what I might inadvertently let slip and so I thanked the doctor politely and turned his offer down.

The only thing that helped me heal was the house. It settled quietly around me, holding me in its heart, bolstering me until I was strong enough to stand on my own again. Strong enough to continue my labours. Strong enough to face whatever lay ahead.

Eight

Louise put her hand up to her cheek, relieved to feel the soft unblemished skin under her touch. She had become so involved in Matilda's world, that she had physically felt Matilda's pain. Matilda was fast becoming the friend Louise hadn't had in a long time. In over 20 years, Louise realised. With her head leaning against the armchair and her hands caressing the book, she let her mind drift back in time.

Louise's father had been in the armed forces. More specifically the British Army. He'd believed in the system, was brought up in the system and naturally assumed she was happy within the system. Being in the system in those days meant being sent away to boarding school as she grew up, as her parents travelled around the world. The British Army in their infinite wisdom recognised that it was not always a good thing for children to be dragged around the world after their parents, or more specifically, after their fathers. They therefore paid for much of the cost of boarding school. There were opportunities for weekly boarding as well as full time boarders, but her father being one of those men who thought children should be seen and not heard, felt that termly boarding would be best, meaning that Louise was neither seen, nor heard.

As a result she had always been a rather solitary child. Other children in the schools she went to came from rich parents. Hers were not so much rich, as self-important. The other kids tolerated her, which was all she could say about them really. They weren't unkind, just uncaring. She wasn't bullied or picked on. The other children just didn't seem to see her most of the time. It was as if she were a waif, or a ghost. There, yet unseen. There, merely tolerated. There, but mostly ignored.

And then one day life at boarding school changed. For Trudy arrived. Trudy was from the same military background as Louise and as a result they found they knew the same places, had lived on the same garrisons, understood the system and each other's way of life. They were both lost souls trailing along in the wake of their parents. For Louise it meant that suddenly life was better, the sun hotter, colours brighter, food tastier. Louise began to realise that she'd been living a shadow of a life before Trudy came along.

They had two happy years together, but then returning one September after the long summer holidays, for what was to be her last year at school, Louise hadn't been able to find her friend. Trudy wasn't in their dorm room when Louise went to unpack. Rushing off to find her, Louise pushed though groups of squealing girls, their voices becoming higher pitched with each friend found. She tripped over trunks and sports equipment, watched as parents said goodbye to their offspring, the mothers often being more upset than their child at the parting. Uniform green sweaters and tartan skirts were everywhere, but none of them were worn by Trudy. Louise staggered back to the dorm room, her excitement draining, as her fear rose. Trudy's bed in the dorm room was still empty. Unable to look at the symbol of her disappointment, Louise curled up in a ball on her own bed and scrunched her eyes shut. She tried not to cry, but couldn't help herself. She was plain scared. Where was Trudy? Why wasn't she here? Louise stayed curled up on top of her bed, until someone shook her on the shoulder.

'You, Louise?' the girl said and without waiting for an answer continued, 'The Headmistress wants to see you.'

Louise climbed off the bed and stumbled her way through the maze of corridors and stairs, until she reached the Headmistress' office, where she was ushered in at once and told to sit on the hard backed chair in front of the desk. Louise did as she was told. Not knowing what to do with her hands, she sat on them, pinning them down, trying to get some semblance of control over her body, which was squirming with fear.

'I understand you've been asking about Trudy,' the Headmistress said, looking at Louise closely but not unkindly.

'Yes, Headmistress.' Louise screwed up her courage and asked, 'Why isn't she here? Has she been delayed?'

'Louise, I'm afraid there's been some bad news. Trudy won't be coming back to school.'

'Oh, has she gone somewhere else? It's strange that she never told me. Where has she gone? Perhaps I can write to her.'

'No, Louise, Trudy isn't going anywhere else. I'm so sorry, Trudy died in a boating accident whilst on holiday with her parents.'

The Headmistress kept on talking, but Louise no longer heard the words. Instead she looked out of the leaded glass window, saw the clouds obscure the sun, watched the grass wither and fade to grey and felt the metallic taste of loneliness once more fill her mouth.

Nine

Later, as the evening stretched emptily before her, Louise decided to go shopping at Morrisons, up near the police station in the heart of the new shopping and leisure complex that Aldershot seemed very proud of. There were huge hoardings everywhere in the surrounding areas, extolling the virtues of the centre, encouraging people to go there for shopping, food and entertainment. One benefit of the ever relaxed shop opening hours was that at any time, day or night, you could go to your local supermarket and buy groceries.

When Louise arrived, clad in wool trousers over sensible flat shoes, wool jumper and camel coat, the square was thronged with people and she stood and watched awhile. She saw everyone else enjoying themselves in groups or couples. No one else seemed to be alone, just her. She knew that it was a trick of her mind and that there were probably loads of single people milling around. But the sight of so many human beings crowded into one place made her feel isolated, made her feel that she was the one person there who had no one. Or at least no one who actually wanted to spend any time with her.

She caught sight of herself in a shop window. Her hair was neat and tidy, her green eyes beautifully made-up although a little dull looking and her clothes sensible. Well, nondescript if she was honest. Good cut, well made, but without any 'life' in them. It was easier to say what they weren't rather than what they were. She turned this way and that. They weren't flamboyant. They weren't sexy. But then again, they weren't trashy. But nor were they particularly fashionable. She caught someone looking at her strangely and moved away from the glass window. She heard Peter in her head, saying that she mustn't make a spectacle of herself and so headed for the Morrisons supermarket to do her shopping.

After collecting a trolley, she mechanically walked the aisles of the supermarket, putting foodstuff in her trolley whilst on automatic pilot. Buying what she always bought for the weekly shopping. What she would buy again next week and the week after that, ad infinitum. That evening she fancied none of the usual tasty treats that normally tempted her. She was indifferent to the donuts, fruit or custard, which were normally a firm favourite. The smell of the cooked chickens from the roasting spit for once made her feel nauseous instead of hungry.

Time spent in the queue to pay seemed endless, her depression deepening with every couple she saw kissing, or mother laughing at her baby's antics. Then at last she was free of the supermarket and pushing the unwieldy trolley in front of her, she trudged back to the car. She filled the boot with overflowing carrier bags and once the trolley was returned and her pound coin safe in her pocket, she climbed into her car and drove out of the car park.

Shivering in the cold as she waited patiently for a gap in the traffic, she looked down at the controls of her small black Mercedes A7. She found the correct lever and turned the heating up high. As she raised her eyes to the road again, she saw her husband drive past in his Lexus. The sight of him made her feel as though she had been drenched with cold water, the shock of it leaving her unable to breathe. What was he doing? He should be in the Mess enjoying dinner or a few drinks with his cronies. He hadn't actually said what the occasion was, but he had definitely told her he would be in the Mess and not to wait up.

Recklessly pulling out into the stream of traffic, ignoring the angry car horns and narrowly missing an Audi, she began to follow him.

Ten

Peter eased the Lexus around the corner into the industrial estate. Yesterday he'd heard some of the lads boasting about their exploits with certain ladies of the night. He'd pretended not to hear their barrack-room raucous stories, but was, in fact, paying close attention. He'd learned where the best girls could be found, how much they charged and the increased sexual excitement that came from the fear of being found out.

'The wife would have my guts for garters if I did anything like that,' one said.

'Ah well then, the trick would be not to get found out wouldn't it?'

'Don't think I need anything like that,' one particularly barrel-chested soldier replied. 'My wife's too hot to handle as it is. I don't have any spare energy left!'

Much was made of the man's bragging and Peter found himself blushing at their banter, even though he wasn't part of the conversation, even though he was hidden behind a vehicle. How easily they talked of their sexual exploits, described the girls they'd bedded and recounted tales of those who had turned them down. He envied them their freedom of actions and freedom of speech. He often wished he wasn't quite so straight laced, quite such an officer, quite 'the old man', the Colonel who they all looked up to.

And so, for once in his boring predictable life, he'd decided to do something about it. He would go and see for himself. He wanted to find out if the lads were exaggerating, to see if the girls were even remotely attractive. He wasn't going to do anything. Oh no. He just wanted to watch. He'd told Louise he was busy at the Mess, which gave him plenty of time to reconnoitre. He told himself he was doing this so he could understand the men under his command better, to try and get a handle on what made them tick. So that he'd be able to picture in his mind the girls and the area they were talking about when they had a good natured go at each other.

The industrial estate roads were dark and unfriendly as his car purred along. He was cocooned in the luxury, surrounded by leather seats and walnut dashboard, with classical music playing softly in the background. He was startled out of his reverie by the sudden lamp-lit road he came across. Panicking he pulled over on the opposite side of the road, the engine still running, his hands damp on the steering wheel. Stood under the lights he could see a line of women. Back-lit from the street lights, their features were fuzzy, until a car drove along the line, illuminating them one by one, until the customer made his choice and pulled up to allow a girl to get into the car.

Peter pressed gently on the accelerator, crossing the road and easing the car over to them. He allowed his gaze to rove over the women as he drove alone the line. They were short, tall, blond, brunette, big chested, small chested, long legged, big bottomed, young and old women and girls. The sight literally took his breath away. There was something here for everyone. Every taste was catered for.

When he reached the end of the line and the road was once more plunged into darkness, he stopped his car. There were beads of sweat on his forehead and his breathing was irregular. He'd had no idea it was that easy to find a girl. To find a girl who would do most anything, for the right price. The price didn't bother him, he had plenty of money. What drew him to them and excited him, were the sexual possibilities. There would be no thrill of the chase, but he had never been any good at that sort of thing. As his men had said, instead there would be the thrill of getting caught. The danger of being seen by someone from the garrison, recognised by another soldier, or even by his wife. Although the red light area was the last place he expected to find Louise.

Peter squirmed in the leather driver's seat and clenched and unclenched his grip on the steering wheel. He couldn't do it. He should go home. Leave well alone. Go back to Louise. But the thought of his wife hardened his resolve. Maybe he could give it a go. He wondered what it would be like to have someone do what he wanted them to do, with no questions asked. He could be given a blow job. Bury his face in large breasts. Fondle a willing bottom. The possibilities were endless.

Without any conscious thought, he followed the desires of his body. He turned the car around and drove back to the line of girls. He looked up and down until he found the one he wanted. As he stopped beside her, she leaned into his car through the open window and said, 'Hi, fancy a bit of fun?'

He remembered very little after that, as he gave himself over to his excitement.

Eleven

It was nearly midnight when Peter returned home last night. Louise knew because she had still been awake, but he hadn't realised that. She'd kept her breathing soft and slow and willed her body not to react to the cold air and freezing feet he'd brought to bed with him. She must have pulled it off, for he fell asleep beside her within minutes. But then she guessed he would have been tired after his sexual exertions. She knew exactly where Peter had been last night and it wasn't the Officers' Mess as he'd told her. She'd followed him, hanging a few cars back, until he'd turned onto the perimeter road of an industrial estate. Confused, Louise had continued to track him and when he pulled over to the side of the road, she stopped as well.

From the opposite side of the street, sitting in her dark car, she'd watched him slowly cruise past a line of barely dressed girls strung out along the pavement. When he'd stopped next to one, the girl had leaned into the car and started to talk to him. Talk to her husband. She'd wanted to scream out loud, to tell the girl to fuck off, to tell Peter to get himself back home. Instead, giving into her breeding and conditioning, Louise had bent her head to rest on the steering wheel and closed her eyes, only opening them after she'd heard his car door open, then close and the sound of his engine pulling away. She hadn't followed him after that as she hadn't wanted to see further evidence of his infidelity. So she'd driven home, tears streaming down her face.

Once there, she'd mechanically unpacked the shopping, made a cup of tea and taken it to bed. But she hadn't drunk it, merely burrowed under the bed covers, hiding from the world, her marriage and her husband. More than anything else she'd wanted to erase the memory of what she'd seen. But she couldn't. The images were looping over and over again in her head, as she examined them as closely as police examine CCTV footage. She couldn't get rid of the sounds of that blatant, flirty girl, that woman, that whore, leaning into Peter's car and then driving away with him. Giving into her emotions, she'd screamed her hurt and rage into the pillow.

The following morning at breakfast, still dressed in her silk pyjamas and matching dressing gown, Louise was all sweetness and light, pouring on the charm as she poured the tea from the pot to refill Peter's cup. When she asked how his evening had gone, he persisted with the lie that he'd been at the Officers' Mess for hours.

'Darling, you wouldn't believe how monotonous it was,' he said, then took a sip of his tea.

'Poor you. Tell me all about it,' she replied, buttering her toast. 'Who was there?'

'No one you know.'

'Well, what did you talk about for all those hours?'

'Nothing to worry your head about,' he said, folding up the newspaper he had been reading. Glancing at his watch he pushed his chair away from the table.

'Anyway, I must be off,' he said as he left the kitchen.

A few minutes later he called from the hall, 'See you tonight,' and with a bang of the front door, he was gone.

She stood in the kitchen, bewildered. Peter had just acted as though nothing had happened last night. He was obviously determined to keep his filthy little secret, wouldn't any husband? But what should she do about it? Louise had been thinking about that most of the night, lying next to a sleeping Peter. Once her anger and hurt had subsided, she'd tried to analyse her problem and think logically about it, tried to come up with a plan to deal with it. But she hadn't managed it. She'd eventually fallen asleep out of pure exhaustion.

She walked into the hall and stared at the closed front door. The clock in the hall startled her by announcing it was 9 am. Each striking of the hour reverberated through her and served to bring her back to the present. As the clock struck the ninth note she realised she couldn't dwell on the problems in her marriage, or Peter's dalliance with a prostitute last evening, for that morning duty called.

Louise was used to pushing away emotional problems and getting on with the job, very similar to Peter, she supposed. Her job was being the Colonel's wife. In the army the higher your husband's rank, the more you were expected to be there as a support to him and act as an unpaid welfare officer or social worker for the men and their wives, which tended to preclude a job of one's own.

Today she was meeting the Welfare Officer. But before that she had to meet the Regimental Sergeant Major's wife for coffee. In the informal hierarchy among army wives the two queen bees in the hive were usually the Colonel's lady and the RSM's wife, who between them exerted a lot of informal power. Although Louise had never seen her position as one of power, she took her responsibility as the Colonel's wife seriously. So she changed gears from spurned wife in her personal life, into the Colonel's wife in her working life, and went upstairs to dress.

As she drove through the garrison, she looked at the other wives out and about. Some were walking into town in twos and threes, with little ones in tow. Groups of women were chatting to each other as they shopped for bits and pieces at the NAFFI shop. What struck Louise about them was that they were all unconstrained. Not hindered as she was by her position as the Colonel's wife, they could flaunt their sexuality. Even though they were in the company of women, they still wore their signature low cut tops, or figure hugging dresses, or skirts as short as belts. She looked down at her own clothes, which were staid by comparison and wondered if that was why Peter preferred other women to her.

Her informal meeting with Claudia Knight was like a prelude to her meeting with the Welfare Officer. Claudia was an excellent RSM's wife, she was sensible, down to earth and unflappable in an emergency. After pouring Louise a coffee, Claudia sat opposite her on a matching settee.

'You've done a great job of settling in, Claudia,' Louise said, looking around the home that had just the sort of atmosphere she had hoped to achieve in her own and failed. The settees were large and comfortable, adorned with scatter cushions that Louise sank back against. Claudia's rugs were vibrantly coloured and shaggy, not muted and short piled. The TV was large and modern with a tangle of wires underneath it, snaking in and out of gaming equipment. There were family photos scattered around the room and on one wall, in pride of place, a black and white photo of the whole family, Claudia, her husband and their two teenage boys. All relaxed and at ease in each other's company wearing broad smiles.

'Thanks, but its second nature by now,' Claudia's eyes crinkled as she smiled at Louise. 'And anyway I quite like it.' She ran her hand through her short cropped blond hair and tucked her legs under her. Legs that were encased in leggings that looked far more comfortable than Louise's woollen trousers.

'Really?' Louise found each move hard and had often wondered how others could possibly welcome it.

'Yes, it means I've a chance for a complete change every couple of years, blowing out the cobwebs, if you like. I know my furniture is mostly the same but the house I put it in is different. And each posting allows for more possibilities.'

'Really?'

'Yes, new people, new town, new facilities, I love it.'

'Well good for you,' Louise said pushing away the green monster of envy, then turned the conversation onto safer subjects. 'How about the ranks? Is everyone alright? Is there anything I should know about before I see the Welfare Officer this afternoon?'

'They're pretty much okay. A couple of the lads are getting married soon and there seems to be a problem with accommodation for them. There may be a few who will face financial difficulties, even with the relocation money they get. Some always spend more than they have and I think some of them may need a loan against their wages. But morale is good and most of them seem glad to be home.'

Louise grabbed a notebook out of her bag and made notes as Claudia spoke. Even though the meetings with the Welfare Officer were confidential, Louise often helped by taking some of the requests for help to other closely aligned agencies. At other times, it could just be a case of a little visit to a family and lending a supportive ear. The work was rather akin to being a bit of a counsellor, she supposed.

As Louise reluctantly got ready to leave Claudia's warm and welcoming home, she wondered who counselled the counsellor. If their roles had been reversed and Louise was the RSM's wife, she could, conceivably, have talked to Claudia about her marital problems. The trouble was Louise was at the top of the tree with no safety net.

Twelve

Peter came home for dinner that night and as they ate he chatted about his new posting and promotion. How exciting it was, how he'd inherited a great bunch of lads and that he was positive this was going to be a good move for them. He asked after her day and Louise told him of her meeting with the RSM's wife and the Welfare Officer, leaving out her envious feelings about Claudia Knight's home. Peter seemed pleased that she was taking up the mantel, as he put it, but in truth he was clearly more interested in the personal troubles currently befalling his men, than any troubles Louise might have. When she haltingly tried to tell him of her nervousness he passed it off as something that she'd soon get used to. He urged Louise to make good on her promise to help his lads, for happy soldiers made for good soldiers.

After their meal Peter grabbed the remote control for the television and Louise excused herself, saying she fancied a nice bath and would then read in bed.

Studying her figure in the bathroom mirror afterward, all pink and glowing from the hot water, she found it still trim, unmarked and attractive. Maybe the problem wasn't on the inside, but on the outside, she mused. Maybe the problem was her clothes. Perhaps she just didn't look sexy enough. Walking into the bedroom, she picked out of a drawer a silky 'teddy' that she had bought on a whim but never had the courage to wear. As she fingered the iridescent material, she came to a decision. She'd take a risk. For surely if she looked like the type of woman Peter picked up from the street, then he'd be more open to the charms of his wife.

She was looking at herself in the mirror, dressed in the provocative lingerie when he entered the room. She'd failed to realise that she could no longer hear the muted sounds of the television filtering up from downstairs. Startled, she quickly composed herself and turned to him and smiled. She guessed it was now or never.

'What do you think, darling?' she asked, once again looking at herself in the mirror, turning this way and that. Then moving to him, she slipped her arms around his waist and began nuzzling his neck. 'Do you want to make love tonight?' she whispered against his skin and kissed it. 'It's been ages.' Kiss. 'Do you like what I'm wearing?' Kiss.

Slowly she began to realise that Peter wasn't moved by her advances, wasn't responding. He hadn't put his arms around her. He wasn't kissing her.

Taking a step backwards and dropping her arms, she asked, 'Darling, what's wrong?' for the man in front of her didn't look like her husband.

Peter was standing stock still, his body rigid, his fists clenched, staring at her. He was radiating not heat and lust but coldness and was looking at her with something approaching hatred in his eyes. Louise took another step backwards, her hands grasping and finding the dressing table behind her. The look in his eyes frightened her. It was as if her Peter had been replaced by someone entirely different. Someone who didn't recognise his own wife. Someone she didn't recognise as her husband.

'Look at yourself,' he said and in those words she could hear his contempt for her. Her legs, suddenly unable to bear the weight of her body, threatened to snap like twigs. But then he grasped her arms and jerked her upright. Turning her around he held her head, making her look at herself in the mirror. 'What do you see?' he hissed into her ear.

But she couldn't answer. She was too afraid. His voice wasn't filled with love, it was overflowing with venom. She bit the inside of her cheek to dampen down the cry that was building inside her chest, stopping her breathing.

Still holding her, Peter pointed at the mirror. 'Do you know what I see? I see a dried, shrivelled up, barren excuse for a woman.'

Louise closed her eyes against both the image and his words. Then jerked them open again as Peter grabbed a heavy perfume bottle from the dressing table and threw it at the mirror. The sound of the glass cracking was like an iceberg breaking as it scraped its way through the icy sea. Now all she could see were broken images of herself reflected back in the shards of glass. She was a distorted, disfigured woman, dressed in a satin slip, with a macabre slashed face.

'There, that's better,' he said. 'That's more like how I see you,' and he left the room, slamming the door behind him.

Louise continued to stand in front of the mirror, shaking, with tears streaming down her face, until the cold dragged her away from the broken mirror and her cracked image. She shed the lingerie, which now felt abhorrent to her touch and put on warm, familiar pyjamas. She climbed between the cold sheets, where she stayed for the remainder of the night, the sole occupant of their large double bed.

Thirteen

The sun streaming into the bedroom from the window woke Louise the next morning. She patted the bed behind her, but there was no one there. Struggling to free herself from the befuddlement of sleep and tangle of sheets, she sat up, confirming that she was alone in the bedroom. The bedclothes on Peter's side were undisturbed. Louise had spent a good deal of time crying last night, muffling the sound with her pillow. She knew Peter didn't like it when she cried. He found it difficult to deal with outward displays of emotion. He often said that it wasn't that he didn't feel any emotion, just didn't feel the need to let everyone see it. And so her tears only seemed to make his resolve to ignore her pain, harden. She'd known he wouldn't return to their bedroom if he heard her sobs, but she hadn't been able to help herself, she couldn't stop the tears, she'd been unable to hold in her sadness.

She shuffled to the bathroom and bathed her red, sore eyes with cold water before going downstairs, where she found Peter in the kitchen.

'I've made the tea,' he said, indicating the tea pot, resting on the kitchen table next to an empty cup and the milk jug. 'Must be off, busy day today.'

He pecked her on the cheek and went off to work as though nothing had happened the previous night. Nothing at all. Louise couldn't get her head around it. Where had his anger gone? Was it still there, but buried somewhere deep inside him? Or had it disappeared as quickly as it had come and he'd been too embarrassed to face her last night?

His angry words had clearly been a reference to her inability to have children. When they'd realised there was a problem with Louise conceiving, they'd embarked on the path of finding a solution. However, the doctors had never really come up with a definitive diagnosis of Louise's problems. It was established that there was nothing wrong with Peter, so it must be her. But years of tests and fertility treatments had all been in vain, the treatments proved as unproductive as her body.

Louise had been surprised by her inability to get pregnant. To her it was just a given. Get married. Have children. What could be simpler? It was the same with her marriage to Peter. Somehow that became a given over the years of their courtship as well. When Peter had proposed, she had been expected to accept. In everyone's minds there was no alternative. It was just something she would do. It was her lot in life.

The lack of children had saddened her. Left her as bereft as if she'd had children who had been born and then died. But it had never occurred to her that their relationship would fail because of it. As far as she was concerned marriage was for life. For richer for poorer. In sickness and in health. No one in her family had ever been divorced. And nor would Louise be.

Louise had been very upset for a long time. Liable to burst into tears at any moment over their lack of children. But Peter had seemed more stoical about it, at least on the outside. Never before had he given her an indication that he held her responsible, felt that it was her fault. Louise was very much afraid that her failure to bear Peter children had morphed into a hard, dark mass of hatred for her, buried deep inside of him.

Fourteen

Unable to face the housework, in fact unable to face any chores at all, Louise made a pot of coffee. She then retrieved Matilda's book from its hiding place and once more curled up in the armchair, drink at her elbow and began to read. For she needed a friend and turned to the only one she had. Matilda.....

Being back at home helped me heal, but after a while even the house that had looked after me so well, held no joy for me. I knew I needed to be around people, to get out more. I was becoming isolated, a recluse. But on the other hand, every time I plucked up enough courage to walk down the drive, when I got to the gates I found I was too frightened to leave my sanctuary.

After a while it became clear that I was too self-conscious to go out during the day, least people saw me. Saw my ruined face and were witness to my ruined life. If I could hardly look at myself, how could I inflict that sort of horror on others?

I began to brood on the people that had brought me to this. I had dealt with the first of them and had paid the price for it. But there were more. None of them should be allowed to get away with it. Get away with ruining my life. It was time to decide who should be second on the list. It was time to embark on the next episode in the sad story that was my life.

I walked upstairs, to get this book, to write this entry. As I retrieved the book from its hiding place in my bedroom, I caught sight of myself in the mirror above the dressing table and couldn't stand what I saw reflected in it. So I picked up a shoe and smashed it to pieces. With each crack of the mirror my anger built: anger at my parents for abandoning me and anger at each man who had defiled me. I imagined hitting each one of them as I pounded the mirror with my shoe. Each satisfying 'crack' brought some small semblance of righteous feeling for my cause, as my actions vilified each one of them. No longer could they hurt me. It was time for me to hurt them.

My anger spent, I let the shoe fall to the floor and sank down on the end of the bed. The vile, distorted face I could now see in the mirror was somehow reflective of my inner self. My visage looked broken, bruised and horrific. My hair was wild and damp. My eyes were burning. My clothes disarrayed. I realised I was carrying that anger around with me each day, pent up inside of me. It was time to let it loose. Vengeance would be mine.

Louise considered the short entry. Matilda was searching for those whom she felt should pay for the person she had become, those who had made her the way she was and Louise thought that it was an interesting concept. Events in Matilda's life had left her angry, bitter, resentful and vengeful. Which were just the same feeling that Louise had. But who should pay for the way Louise was feeling? Who was responsible for luring her husband away from her? Who was her husband turning to, instead of his wife? The answer popped into her head at once. It was startlingly clear. So obvious that she wondered why she had not realised it before, for a blind man could have seen it. It was obviously his prostitute.

Louise remembered the girl who had leaned into her husband's car. She'd never be able to get that image out of her head. She saw it every time she looked at Peter. The girl's breasts dangling through the open window into the Lexus, so that they were nearly touching his face. Her arse stuck out with a skirt so short it didn't cover her pants. Blond hair caught up in a twist. Red painted lips that promised so much. Louise wondered if they were true to that promise and that Peter been satisfied by her.

Louise walked to the cellar, to return the book to its hiding place. Peter hadn't mentioned the mirror he'd broken last night and neither had she. It was still there, in the bedroom, hanging on the wall, useless and broken. She must clear it up. After collecting an empty cardboard box and grabbing a pair of gardening gloves, she climbed the stairs to the bedroom, each tread on the stairs taking her closer to Peter's words and actions. Taking her back to last night. She paused at the bedroom door, tears filling her eyes. She brushed them away impatiently. She really must stop being so emotional and become as controlled and contained as her husband. With a deep breath, she turned the handle, opened the door and walked over to the broken mirror. She carefully teased the shards of glass out of the frame, putting them in the box. All the while, running through her head, were the words Peter used to describe her; dried, shrivelled up, barren.

Once the frame was empty of glass, she took it outside and leant it up against the bin. Returning to the house, she collected the cardboard box from the bedroom, intending to take that to the bin as well. But before taking it outside, she opened the box and looked at the shards of glass inside. She thought about Matilda.

She thought about Peter. She thought about the prostitute. Then she thought that it was just possible she could find a use for the glass. So she closed the lid and decided to store it in the cellar, next to where the book was hidden.

Fifteen

Peter was getting ready to go away on a three day exercise. All his perfectly ironed clothes were rolled up and stowed away in his kit bag, which was lying on the bed.

'Got everything?' she asked him from the doorway, where she'd been watching him, unobserved.

'I think so,' he paused for a moment, thinking. 'Bugger, my shaving kit, it's in my wash bag, can you get it?'

Louise nodded and went into the bathroom, retrieving the bag he kept in the cupboard under the sink. He only ever used it when he was away, preferring an electric shave whilst he was at home. If he did shave on exercise, it was usually a dry shave with a blade, several of which were in the small bag. It also contained a flannel, soap, toothbrush and toothpaste.

'Here,' she said handing it to him on her return.

He placed it on top of the rest of his gear, drew the bag closed and took it with him down the stairs. She followed him like a puppy who knew something was going on, but wasn't sure what and was staying close to her master for reassurance.

Peter placed the bag on the floor by the door and turned to her, pulling her close and kissing her cheek. She breathed in the smell of him. The musky odour of the man she loved who rejected her day after day.

'Sorry, about, well, you know,' he said referring to his behaviour the other day: his hateful words, the broken mirror, her broken spirit. It was the first time he'd mentioned it since the incident. He tucked his hand under her chin and tilted her head so she had no option but to look at him. 'It's just this promotion,' he said. 'I'm a bit stressed, that's all. You do understand don't you?'

Louise didn't, but nodded her agreement when he let go of her chin.

'I'm doing this for both of us, you know. Climbing the old ladder of promotion,' he said, attempting a smile, but it had very little warmth in it.

She still didn't believe him, but managed a small smile in return.

'Good girl,' he said. 'Don't want you upset while I'm away,' and with a final kiss on her lips, he hoisted his bag and was gone.

She stood in the hall, looking at the closed door. At least he'd apologised, she supposed. But she didn't really believe he'd meant it. His words seemed glib, empty of the emotion they were meant to express. She knew the reasons behind his words and knew that they were more for him than her. Peter needed reconciliation so she'd not go anywhere whilst he was away. So he didn't have to worry and could give his full attention to the exercise, which probably consisted of a lot of soldiers getting lost in the middle of nowhere for hours on end. He needed to ensure she'd continue being the Colonel's wife, acting as surrogate mother to the wives of the men who were with him. He needed to be confident that she would continue to do her duty in his absence.

She knew Peter needed her by his side. He might not want her body at the moment, but she was certainly necessary as his wife, for he'd so wanted the promotion and she was part of the reason he'd got it. But he needn't worry. She wouldn't leave him, for she had nowhere else to go.

She wandered into the kitchen to make a cup of tea that she didn't really want. It was more for something to do than anything else. As she waited for the kettle to boil she took stock. She had to admit she'd no employable skills. They'd married at an early age, so she'd never worked. Her stuffy old fashioned parents had said that she wouldn't need to work once she had a husband, but in the meantime they supposed she could go to a secretarial college. She often felt her parents were a throwback to a different era. The swinging sixties seemed to have passed them by and instead of moving with the times they were still stuck in the 1950's. But in the end Peter had proposed a few weeks before she was due to start her course. So her parents cancelled her place without telling her. When they eventually confessed, the day before she was due to start, she had felt trapped, but utterly helpless. All she could do was to watch the machine that was Peter, her parents and his parents, as it marched steadily forward and the plans for their wedding began to take shape.

The click of the kettle turning itself off made her jump and she poured the hot water onto a tea bag and went to the fridge. That reminded her that she had no money of her own. Well not enough to be of any use. Peter was in charge of that sort of stuff, giving her a monthly allowance for food, petrol and clothes. She had no one she could to go to either, should she decide to leave him. Her parents were dead and she had no siblings. So she really was trapped. The thought made her shoulders slump, as though burdened by the great weight of her marriage.

Theirs had been a marriage of convenience, on her parent's part at least, she supposed. And she'd gone along with it as though pulled by an invisible string. She seemed too weak to fight against them. She couldn't really blame them, for in the end she supposed she had been complicit. She had walked up the aisle after all and met him at the altar. The saying, marry in haste repent at leisure, made her smile wryly. For now she had no choice but to make the best of it.

And so as she sipped her tea standing by the sink, looking out of the window at the garden, she wondered what to do for the best. How could she make Peter love her again? But what she was really asking herself she realised, was what lengths would she go to, to save her marriage?

Sixteen

As night fell, Louise was ready. She had made her decision, planned carefully and gathered what she needed. All that was left was the execution. She smiled at the double meaning of the word execution. What a mouth-watering, delectable word. She pulled on her black leather gloves and as she backed the small Mercedes out of the garage and drove away, she focused on what mattered. Peter. Peter was all that mattered. She had to save him from those girls, from the false attraction they offered. For what young girl in her right mind would want to sleep with a soldier in his late 40s? Alright so Peter was handsome in that uptight, upper class way of his. But his dark hair was cut in a soldier's style, short with a parting at the side and brushed back off his face. He didn't wear civilian clothes well. He looked out of place in them. He'd worn a uniform for so long that it was like a second skin. When that skin was sloughed off, what was underneath was gawky and self-conscious. But in a uniform he was in command, in charge and confident. A different man altogether.

Louise saw the industrial estate looming out at her

from the darkness and the line of girls waiting to fleece the men who came along, charging twenty quid for a quickie, or at least as quick as they could make it happen. She was sure none of them wanted to linger with a customer for long. While you were chatting, they were losing money. So no street girl would want to waste time.

She wondered if Peter realised that and just wanted the physical release. She had never thought him a stupid man. But then again, maybe he was. If anyone found out his little secret, he would be belittled in the eyes of his men and frowned upon by those higher up the chain of command and he wouldn't want that. So it was up to Louise to save him from himself.

As she slowly drove along the line, she couldn't see the girl she was looking for at first. There were some blonds there, but with short hair, not long blond hair tied back. Most of them had red lips and breasts on display and Louise began to wonder if the girl she was seeking was working that night. Or maybe she was already with a customer. And then she saw her, right near the end of the line. Louise exhaled loudly with relief and pulled up next to her.

The girl leaned into the car window, just as she had done a few nights ago at Peter's car, when she had leaned in and tempted him. The prostitute must have been shocked to find a woman in the car, for a small, 'Oh!' escaped her lips.

'You don't mind women, do you?' Louise asked. 'I'm prepared to pay the going rate.'

The working girl shrugged. 'Suppose not,' she said.

'Hop in then,' Louise leaned over and opened the car door for her.

As soon as the girl was in Louise drove away,

immediately heading for open country. 'Let's drive out of town. It's a lovely night. How about Badshot Lea? It'll be quiet there. I've got a rug in the back.'

'Whatever,' the girl shrugged and put her hand on Louise's leg. Trying not to flinch from the touch, Louise offered a fake smile and pushed hard on the accelerator. They soon reached their destination, a small wooded area with public access that Louise had picked out. Parking the car by the side of a track, Louise sprang out and grabbed the rug from the boot and struck out, climbing over the style. 'Come on,' she called. 'Just in here.'

By the time the girl arrived at Louise's chosen spot, the rug was already laid out and Louise was sitting on it. She lay down and patted the space next to her.

'Look at those stars,' Louise said. 'Aren't they beautiful?'

'Suppose,' the girl replied lying on her back beside Louise and looking up at the night sky. 'It's extra for women you know.'

'Don't worry,' said Louise, turning on her side and leaning over the girl. 'I've plenty of money.'

Louise didn't give herself any time to think, or speak, for actions spoke louder than any words could. The prostitute opened her mouth, but anything she had been about to say died on her lips, as Louise plunged the shard of glass she had brought with her from the broken mirror at home, straight through the girl's right eye.

'That'll teach you to sleep with my husband,' Louise whispered in the girl's ear. She wasn't sure if her victim could hear her anymore. But it was of no matter. The deed was done and Peter was free of her. The eye the prostitute had left, gazed sightlessly at the night sky as the stars continued to look down on the two women, unchanged and untroubled by what Louise had just done.

Not wanting to leave any potential evidence behind, Louise grabbed the rug, lifting one end so the girl rocked off it and came to rest on the grass on her back. The girl's shoe had fallen off as she'd rolled, so Louise picked it up and put it back on the limp foot. Bundling the fleecy wool rug in her arms, she returned to the car, without so much as a backward glance. As she started the engine, she realised there was blood on her driving gloves. Peeling them off she decided she would discard them with the rug. She wasn't worried as both items were replaceable. It was her husband that wasn't.

Seventeen

The military detective, Sgt Major Crane, picked his way across the muddy field. The early morning mist was dissipating but was leaving behind dew which was stubbornly clinging onto his short curly black hair. He ran his hand over it and rubbed away the dampness, then wiped his palms on his black raincoat to dry them. As he walked, Crane cursed the field, the weather and DI Anderson of the local Aldershot Police, who had seen fit to get him out of his warm bed at some unearthly hour in the morning and into a field that looked like it had been used for an army exercise. Police cars, an ambulance and forensic vans were parked here there and everywhere, forcing Crane onto the damp grass to get away from the mud churned up by the car tyres. He wondered for the third time why he hadn't put on his wellingtons when he'd parked his car on the roadside. Oh great, he'd just trodden in a patch of mud that looked suspiciously like a cow pat, which he fervently hoped it wasn't.

His inspection of the muddy mess around his feet and clinging to his shoes was interrupted by Anderson calling, 'Crane, over here! What's keeping you?'

'Coming, Derek,' Crane called and as he drew near to the policeman he said, 'Please tell me there's a good reason for me being here at this ungodly hour.'

'Good morning to you too, Crane,' Anderson replied. 'Got a nasty one here,' and inclined his head in the direction of a white plastic tent that had been erected just a few feet away from them.

'Is nasty the reason you called? Just to share? I know we're friends, but this is above and beyond.'

'Shut up, Crane and listen. Here, coffee might help your mood,' and Anderson grabbed a paper cup of coffee from a passing uniformed constable and handed it to Crane. 'Don't know what you're moaning about, I've been here most of the night, so you've had more sleep than me. Right,' Anderson turned towards the tent. 'Young woman, killed sometime last night. Found by some kids messing around in what's known locally as 'lover's lane'. They were hoping to wind-up some couples looking for a bit of peace and quiet, if you get my meaning and they ended up getting a bit more than they bargained for.'

'You mean people voluntarily come all the way out here to this God forsaken spot? It's not exactly scenic.' Crane looked around at the landscape, which comprised mostly of bare spindly trees and muddy farmer's fields.

Anderson ignored Crane's comment and continued, 'One of the cars that responded to the call work the local red light area and the two policemen recognised her as a working girl.' Anderson lifted the flap on the white tent. 'You can go in,' he told Crane. 'Forensics have finished and we're just about to move her. I thought you might like a look before we do. I know you prefer to experience a crime scene yourself, rather than just look at photos.'

Crane handed Anderson his coffee and once inside the tent he stood over the body. The girl was lying on her back, arms outstretched. One side of her face was un-marked with make-up still on. Red lips, dark eyes, pink cheeks, all garish and badly applied. But it was the other side of her face that was the more interesting. For sticking out of her eye socket was a long, thin, shard of glass. Blood had seeped from the wound, trickled down the side of her face and tracked into her hair. Not the most pleasant thing to witness especially before breakfast. Crane squatted down by the girl's head and looked closely at the glass. After a few minutes of thinking and prowling around the lifeless form, looking at her from all angles, he walked out of the tent to join Anderson. Retrieving his coffee, he took a gulp and then said, 'What does the Major say?'

'Major Martin found approximate time of death to be about 10pm. Give or take an hour or so either side.'

'What about the glass? Looking at it, one side was glass, but the other had a backing of some sort.'

'Yes, we think it's from a mirror.'

'And the stuff attached to it?'

'The bits sticking to the jagged edges of the shard, we think could be from a glove, leather, plastic, or some such material. We'll obviously know more once all the forensic tests have been done.'

'Well, it's all very interesting, Derek, but you still haven't told me how the Special Investigations Branch can help.'

Anderson started walking away from the tent and Crane followed him. 'The officers who responded to the call, the ones I told you about, they regularly patrol the working girls' area. Just to make sure there are no problems, you know. We can't keep nicking them every night or we'd never get anything else done. Anyway last night one of the girls flagged them down. She told PC Daniels and his young partner that a friend of hers had gone missing, or rather not returned from going off with a customer. She'd left the line around 9.30pm and hasn't been seen since.'

'So it is more than likely that the customer she went off with could be the bloke who killed her.'

'Seems a reasonable assumption,' Derek agreed nodding. 'But what was interesting was the car she got into.'

'Ah, so this is the punch line is it?'

'So quick, Crane, no wonder you're a detective. Yes, as you say, the punch line is the car. We don't know the make, as mid-sized, dark coloured was about the best the girls could come up with, but apparently the car had a funny number plate.'

Crane stopped walking and peered at Anderson. 'Not a UK number plate?'

'No, the blue bit on it had a letter D then more letters and numbers, but her friend couldn't remember what they were. At first they thought it was Dutch...'

'But it's German,' finished Crane, 'D for Deutschland.'

'Exactly and as Aldershot isn't a favourite UK destination for German tourists, I was just wondering.... do you know anyone who's recently come back from a German posting? Or can you find out for me? But first, we're off to watch the autopsy.'

'Oh joy,' said Crane and stomped off across the field after Anderson.

Eighteen

Crane persuaded Derek that they needed breakfast before facing the autopsy and anyway the Major would need some time to get the girl from the field to the morgue. So as a result it was a much brighter Crane who walked into the autopsy room with Anderson.

'Morning, you two,' called Major Martin, a retired army pathologist, who had joined the team based at Frimley Park Hospital upon leaving the forces. 'Glad you're here, I'm just getting to the interesting bit.'

'That being?'

'The glass in her eye, we've taken all the photos and it's time to get it out of her.'

Major Martin turned back to the body. Crane watched as the doctor leaned over her. The young girl, who was once a vital, alive, human being, lay displayed on the metal table. But no longer displayed for their entertainment so to speak, considering her profession. Now she was displayed in order that her body could give up the secrets of her death.

The Major grabbed what looked like a pair of pliers and clasped them around the top of the glass shard.

'Now,' he said, 'I really want to get this out in one

piece. Jim, hold her head would you?'

Major Martin's diminutive assistant moved around to the end of the table and grasped the girl's head in his hands, holding them either side of her skull, his fingers laced in her hair.

'Okay, here we go. I'm hoping to do this slow and steady, Jim, so keep a good hold of her head.'

Crane watched fascinated as the piece of glass was slowly drawn out of the girl's eye. The orb gave up its prize with a sucking sound, which sounded rather too much like a baby suckling on a teat for Crane's liking. The glass was covered in blood and other bits of goo and Crane asked what they were.

'Ah,' said the Major in reply. 'Well, it's probably easiest if I explain what happens when you poke something into the eye.' Pretending to stab himself in his own eye, he said, 'The glass would firstly pierce the lens with ease, pass through the aqueous humor (eye jelly) and through the retina and more than likely end up fairly far into the brain, finishing about 1 to 2 inches from the back of the skull if you were using something this long.'

The Major brandished the piece of glass in Crane's face, rather too close for comfort and with rather too much gusto for Crane's liking. 'It's at least 9 inches long. So on this we can see blood, eye jelly and brains. But there are other materials on this, I reckon.'

The Major placed the shard in a long specimen tray and looked at it through a hand magnifier. 'I'll know more later once we've done the tests, but for instance there could be grass, mud and such on it, considering where the girl was found.'

'Would she have died instantly?' Crane asked.

'Pretty much.'

'A small mercy,' said Anderson.

A sentiment Crane agreed with.

Crane and Anderson turned to leave, after a promise from Major Martin to give Anderson his full findings as soon as possible. As they trudged across the car park to their respective cars, Crane lit a cigarette.

'Pretty nasty this one, Derek,' he said, blowing out a lungful of smoke.

'Yes,' Anderson agreed, walking along with his hands in the pocket of his tweed jacket that he wore underneath a well-worn beige raincoat, reaffirming Crane's impression of the fictional detective Columbo. All that was needed was a cigar, but Anderson was a staunch non-smoker.

'Hasn't Mrs Derek made you throw that out yet?' he asked poking at Anderson's raincoat.

'She keeps trying, but I keep finding it. You know I found it for sale in a charity shop once,' he laughed.

'What did you do?'

'Bought it, of course,' and the two men chuckled their way back to their cars. 'Seriously, Crane, find out about soldiers returning from Germany, won't you? It's the only thing we have at the moment, especially if Major Martin comes up a blank on any forensic evidence on the glass itself.'

'Will do,' Crane replied. 'Where are you off to?'

Before Anderson could reply, a text message appeared on his phone. After reading it, he looked back at Crane, 'Back into town. The girl has been named as Sally Smith and we've an address, it's a room over one of the pubs.' Anderson put the phone back in his pocket. 'I doubt it will tell us anything. My gut feeling is she was killed by a punter.'

'An anonymous killer will make our job harder.'

'Exactly, but I like your use of the words, 'our job'. I'll hold you to that, Crane. See you later.'

As Anderson climbed into his car, Crane stubbed out his cigarette underfoot and climbed into his own vehicle. Watching Anderson's car drive away, Crane scratched at the scar under his short, sharply cut, dark beard that he'd been given permission to grow to cover it up. As he scratched, he thought about the ways he could find out about German plated cars and returning soldiers. Staff Sgt Jones was his best bet. He was the man in operational charge of the military police and guards. Every car on the garrison had to be logged, with details recorded of the owner, registration number and make.

1976

Headmaster Thaddeus Brown closed and locked the main door to his school with relief. He turned away from it and then leant his back against it, surveying his domain. Once empty of teachers and pupils, the school settled down to rest and wait for the next onslaught tomorrow morning. He could hear the creak of its tired old rafters and sigh of the floorboards as if they were saying, thank goodness, peace at last, which was pretty much the same way Thaddeus felt. He was simply exhausted and, he believed, ready to retire. It wasn't so much the work that tired him out, the management of the staff and the school budget, it was the children. Each year a new intake of exuberant, vocal young ones raised his excitement level. He was too old to take the strain of it anymore. The pressure he felt when he had to force himself to keep his hands off them.

Pushing himself off the door, his tweed-clad legs and brogue covered feet walked the long corridors. He poked his head into classrooms, occasionally opening a desk drawer, or a cupboard. Not prying as such, he was just keeping his finger on the pulse of the school.

He was pleased by the classrooms that celebrated the children's work and disgruntled by the ones of other teachers who hadn't taken as much care. Cupboards with supplies spilling out displeased him and he made a mental note to talk to the teachers responsible for the mess. Walking into the main hall, he smelled the intoxicating aroma of sweaty young bodies and boiled cabbage. He looked at a display of photographs from the recent drama production which Year 6 had given to the whole school. He peered closely at their photographs, seeing the changes in some of his favourite charges, as they had grown from 4 years to their now 11 years of age.

How he loved his children, cherished them, revered them. The trouble was, not everyone agreed with his adoration and what he did to the children most special to him. It should have been their secret, his and the child's. But some of the recent intake of little ones hadn't quite seen it that way. He realised that times were a-changing and now even four and five year-olds had voices that were being heard, where once they hadn't.

And so, it seemed, he was to resign, before those voices got louder, before they became a swell that he could not ignore. That the Governors could not ignore. He intended to tell the governing body tonight. Not about his predilection, but to announce that he was retiring. After all he was over 60 and he would say that it was time to let the younger generation take over.

He prepared the hall for the meeting of the school governors, setting out tables and chairs and then retired to his office to await his fate. He rather thought he needed a bit of Dutch courage and he had a bottle of whisky hidden in the bottom of a filing cabinet, for just such an occasion as this. Retrieving it, he poured a finger full into the glass and returned the bottle to its hiding place, so that he wouldn't be tempted to have another and another and another. For that's how he felt tonight, wanting the warming sensation of the whisky as it slid down his throat into his stomach. Needing the alcohol to dull his senses just enough to take the edge off any allegations the Governors might make this evening.

As he sipped his drink, he thought about his children, who would keep him company in the coming years. Years that stretched emptily before him.

Nineteen

Did that shock you, dear reader? The fact that it was a parish priest who first abused me? How could a man of the cloth reconcile the atrocities he was committing with his faith, with the preaching of Jesus? The Son of God wanted communities to look after their children. How does the phrase go? 'Suffer little children to come unto me.' It appears my parish priest took some of those words too literally. He just turned the phrase around to suit himself. 'Come unto me and suffer.' Oh and here's another titbit of information that is even more shocking. His abuse of me wasn't an isolated incident. It wasn't just me he liked and felt he could partake of as often as he wanted, as though it were his right. He was part of a paedophile ring, a ring that comprised of some surprising local dignitaries. They would take turns. Pass us around like a game of pass the parcel. Once one got tired of me, I would be passed to another who was looking for a young girl.

And so it was that the second disgusting excuse for a man who decided I was the one for him, was the headmaster of the school I attended as a child. He was a figure of authority to me. Parents and children put their trust in him. He was a pillar of the community. What I could never understand was how he stood being surrounded by children every day? Was he sexually excited all the time? What a disgusting thought. What a disgusting man, that he could misuse the trust placed in him that way.

Once I'd decided on my next target, I needed to work out how best to get to him.

Louise closed the book. Peter would be back soon, she saw, looking at her watch. It was time to return the book to its hiding place and then tidy up. As she worked, her movements were mechanical. But her brain was working overtime. For the past two days she'd imagined the police were on their way, poised, ready to knock on her door. They could appear at any time of the day or night. What would they say? What would she say? Had she left anything behind that could identify her? She ran over the events in her mind. She didn't think so. She had pushed the rug and her gloves deep into a large waste bin some miles away from the crime scene. It was very unlikely they would be found.

Louise wondered how Matilda had coped with the aftermath of her first kill. But she hadn't recorded her feelings on the subject. Maybe the disfigurement had overridden any fear of getting caught. She'd had to spend a considerable time recuperating. It was more than likely that had been her focus, rather than thoughts of being uncovered as a killer.

As for herself, Louise had been very jittery since she'd returned home that night. But the fluttering fear was settling down now. The longer she was left alone by the police, the more it seemed she had got away with it. Therefore her overriding feeling, currently, was one of satisfaction. She was convinced she'd done the right thing. Done the right thing for her husband, for he must avoid any scandal that might threaten his career. It was her job, as his wife, to keep things running smoothly and that included their private life. She rubbed her hands together, as if dusting them off, pushing away the vestiges of her crime, wiping her hands clean of them.

And so Louise smiled as she cleaned, sang as she polished and danced as she vacuumed. She had to get the house ready. Clean away the depression still pervading their home with its debilitating tentacles. Banish her fear and sadness. She flung the windows wide, shook out cushions and batted away cobwebs. Peter was due home today and all was right with the world.

Twenty

Crane and Anderson drove through the darkened streets of Aldershot. Crane always thought of the town in terms of black and white. It was a grimy, grainy sort of town, with the odd flash of colour. An urban landscape drained of its life when the Parachute Regiment had moved their base from Aldershot to Colchester in 2003. The skeleton of the town that they left behind was only just beginning to recover from the biggest kick in the teeth it had ever had.

Suddenly the dark night was pierced by street lights and scanned by car headlights. Every few moments there was a flash of flame as someone lit a cigarette. They were in Aldershot's red light area, such as it was. Anderson parked the car and Crane as climbed out, the cold instantly penetrated his suit. He pulled his dark overcoat out of the back of the car and as he shrugged into it, he glanced at the line of girls on the opposite side of the street. All were unsuitably dressed for the cold. Instead of coats and gloves they were wearing what they no doubt perceived to be provocative clothing. From what Crane could see they just looked tacky.

But the two men weren't there to take stock of the wares on sale. Crane and Anderson wanted to talk to the girls themselves. Traffic police officers had passed on snippets of information and the odd comment, which wasn't enough for Anderson. Deciding it would be nigh on impossible to get the girls to come to the police station, he'd invited Crane to accompany him as he questioned the girls while they were at work.

Instantly identifiable as police officers, Crane and Anderson found the girls shrank away from them, melting back into the shadows, unwilling to talk to the enemy in case they were whisked away to the police station. Also none of them wanted to lose money and a police presence was guaranteed to frighten the punters away. Crane knew all this as they walked amongst them, bearing the hatred of their glares, easily shrugging them off his broad shoulders.

As they walked, Anderson spotted the girl he was looking for and nodded for Crane to follow him. Sally Smith's friend, Lindsay, was the only one keen to speak to them and as they approached her, she wanted to know if they'd arrested anyone for her friend's murder yet.

'No, not yet,' Anderson answered her question. 'We're a bit stuck to be honest.'

'Why doesn't that surprise me?'

Crane resented her sarcasm, but supposed he could understand it. Often the public didn't care about the odd prostitute being killed. For they didn't seem to see them as human beings, didn't appreciate that they were someone's daughter, girlfriend or mother even.

'Have you talked to the other girls, like we asked?' Anderson had elicited Lindsay's help yesterday, wanting any observations of the men who regularly, or even intermittently, used their services.

'Yes, but it didn't really get me anywhere. No one seems to have noticed a strange customer. They've not come across one who was aggressive, hurt them, or threatened them. The men were described as mostly sad, old and unwashed, to be honest.'

'Did Sally have any regulars?'

'No, not really,' Lindsay answered Anderson's question. 'Not that I noticed anyway, or not that she talked about.'

'If you do spot anyone who looks a bit dodgy, or hear the other girls talking about a punter who was a bit different, or a bit strange, let me know, will you?' Anderson passed Lindsay his business card. 'And try and get them to remember the make of a car or even the number plates of anyone who is in any way out of the norm.'

'Course,' Lindsay replied and stuffed the card into her bra, the other bits of her clothing not appearing to have any pockets. 'I want her killer caught. I just hope you lot do as well.'

Lindsay held her head up defiantly and walked away going to join the sisterhood she'd signed up to, for a reason known only to herself. Her black, shapely, bobbed hairstyle swung just above her shoulders, in time with her swinging hips and was in sharp contrast to her white painted face and red lips. With her eye catching hairstyle and swaggering attitude, Crane thought she would be easily identifiable from a clutch of similarly dressed girls, which was no doubt her intention. She was flaunting her unique selling point, as it were.

As Crane and Anderson moved away from the girls and crossed the street to go back to Anderson's car, they found they had another girl waiting for them. This time not a working girl, but Diane Chambers, crime correspondent for the Aldershot News. She was casually leaning against Anderson's car and stood up straight at their approach.

'Good evening, Inspector and Sgt Major,' she called, her small digital recorder in her hand as always. 'I wonder if either of you could give me an update on the case,' she said.

'Sorry, Diane,' said Crane. 'There's nothing other than the press release issued earlier today.'

'Which said precisely nothing, Sgt Major, which I take it is what you've got?'

'No comment,' Crane replied. Then softening slightly said, 'Come on, Diane, you know the score.'

'I certainly do,' she said smiling. 'You say nothing and I write what I like.'

Even Crane had to smile at that.

'They're frightened, though, you know,' she said, 'the girls. But they won't stop working, mind you.'

'Neither will we,' Crane said. 'We are continuing to work hard to bring the perpetrator to justice.'

'And that's it? That's my quote?'

'Afraid so, Diane,' Anderson interjected.

'Oh well, I'll just have to ask Billy,' she said impishly, for Diane's boyfriend was none other than Sgt Billy Williams, a member of Crane's Special Investigations Branch team. Although their relationship had been more off than on.

'Ask away, but he's not on this case and even if he was he wouldn't tell you anything.'

'No I know, Crane. It's alright; your Sergeant is safe with me.'

Crane seriously doubted that and thought she was

the least safe person for his young Sergeant to be with. But such was life. Billy was a big boy and old enough to make his own decisions, even if they turned out to be disastrous ones.

Twenty One

Louise decided she wanted to see Peter's reaction when he found out his little prostitute was no more. There had been an article in the local newspaper that day about her murder and Louise thought it would be a good idea to let Peter see it, while she was there. Would he be upset? Or relieved that his little problem had gone away? Would he realise that she had made that happen? Her head was spinning with the possibilities and it was with some relief that she heard his car come down the drive. The time for speculation was over.

She quickly checked her appearance in the mirror. Perfect, as required. She glanced around the downstairs of the house. Also perfect. There was nothing out of place, so Peter wouldn't have any reason to criticise her. All was as it should be in the Colonel's house. She was ready for inspection. A giggle escaped her lips. It came out more manic than light hearted laughter, she realised and she struggled to get a grip of her emotions.

Louise opened the door, watching as Peter climbed out of the car. He glanced up and nodded to her as he grabbed his bag off the back seat. He walked through the door, kissed her perfunctorily on the cheek and dropped his kit on the floor.

'For the wash,' he said. But he didn't take it through to the laundry room and just left it on the floor in the hall. She also ignored the bag and took the opportunity to give him a hug, relishing the male smell of him after three days on exercise and she was pleased and a little relieved if she was honest, when he embraced her back.

As they pulled apart, she said, 'Want some tea? I've just made a pot.'

'Please,' he said and followed her into the kitchen. 'Then I really must have a shower.'

'Yes, you should,' she agreed a smile in her voice. 'So, how did the exercise go?' she asked as he sat down and she handed him a mug.

'Alright, you know,' he said and drew the paper towards him.

'Everyone get back safely?'

'Of course,' he replied as he looked down at the newspaper. She watched as his eyes scanned the page and then stop at the article about the death of a local prostitute. It was short on fact and long on supposition and had been written in an exuberant style by the so called Chief Crime Reporter Diane Chambers.

She watched Peter's expression carefully as he read and drunk his tea. But his face was hard and closed, inscrutable. Then again, it would be for he was a soldier after all. She always reckoned that with that blank expression of his he could have been a detective. At least of the type she'd seen on the television, for she'd never met a police detective in real life.

Later, after their evening meal was eaten and she was clearing the table he said, 'Sorry, darling, I have to go out tonight.'

'Oh,' she said, not really surprised for she had an inkling where he might be going. 'But you've only just got back.'

'I know, but we're having a debriefing tonight. I could be late. Don't wait up. I don't want to ruin your beauty sleep,' he smiled as he went upstairs to get his coat.

Louise was convinced he was going to try and find out about his little prostitute, for she knew that any debriefing would take place tomorrow morning. He'd forgotten she knew the army always held debriefing from exercises the next day. Not the night they arrived back. It was probably the only outward sign she would see of his discomfort. It seemed he wanted to see if the girl who had been killed was the one that he'd liked.

She waved him off from the step of the house before unhurriedly getting her coat and car keys and leaving the house herself. She knew the streets he was heading for. It wouldn't take her long to get there as well, for she wanted to see for herself what he did.

Pulling to a stop on the opposite side of the road to the line of girls, she saw his car was just where she'd expected to find it. Peter seemed to be asking the girls if they knew where someone was. Everyone looked around and then shrugged. But the girls must have woven their poisonous threads around him, for he decided to take another one.

The one he chose had jet black hair, cut into a bob. Was it a wig? Probably, Louise thought, for no whore would be able to afford such a good haircut at least not one standing on the street in an industrial estate in Aldershot. The prostitute he chose wore a top that was cut away at the sides, rather like a trendy bathing suit, showing off her curves and when she bent down Louise could see the girl's stocking tops and suspenders. Such underwear had always been a draw for Peter, although it had been some time since he'd asked Louise to wear them, she realised. After a few moments, whilst they were no doubt haggling over the price, the girl climbed into Peter's Lexus and the whore and her husband roared off down the road.

Twenty Two

Peter kept the pedal to the metal, as the saying went, until they were away from the other girls, heading towards Ash. As they reached The Ranges, Peter pulled into the car parking area, which was deserted. They were alone, with only the sounds of the night for company; the hoot of an owl; the screech of a bat; the rustlings in the undergrowth and the tick, tick, tick, of the metal of his engine as it cooled down.

'You're sure it was her?' Peter turned to look at the girl in the passenger seat. 'It was Sally? She's dead?'

'Yes, sorry, were you a regular?'

Peter shrugged. 'We'd met a few times, I guess. Who do the police think did it?'

'It has to be a punter. She went off with one and was never seen again. She wouldn't have taken off afterwards; she'd have come back to the line. 10 at night would have been far too early to finish. We don't normally clock off until around 2am.'

Peter looked out of the window. He could see the girl reflected in it. 'It's just so horrible that she should have been killed in that way. So pointless,' he said.

He felt a hand on his leg and turned back to her.

'Don't be sad,' she said. 'Sally's probably in a better place now and anyway I'm here. I'll keep you warm,' she smiled beguilingly, her hand travelling up from his knee to his groin.

'I'll do whatever you want,' she leaned forward and whispered, 'I can make you happy,' and her tongue flicked at his ear lobe.

Despite himself, Peter felt a frisson of excitement. He didn't want to, he hadn't imagined that Sally could be so easily replaced. But then again, Lindsay she said her name was, seemed very well practiced in the art of seduction. Her hand was on the move again, finding the buttons of his shirt, undoing them, allowing her fingers to fondle the hairs on his chest. A groan escaped his lips. She unzipped his trousers and he felt her hair flick across him. At which point he was lost. Sanity went out of the window. He turned and reached for her, lowering her car seat so her body lay flat. She shrugged off her top and he eagerly fell on her breasts.

Later, when he dropped Lindsay off, back at the line of girls, she got out of the car and after closing the door, leaned in to speak to him.

'See you again?' she asked her eyes full of mischief and promise.

'Try and stop me,' he grinned as he put the car in gear and pulled away. Although his pleasure with Lindsay was still tinged with sadness about Sally, Peter was relieved that he had so easily found another young girl who was clearly attracted to him. He couldn't believe his luck. As he drove home, he was already planning when he could meet her again.

Louise made her lonely way back to the house. She hadn't dare stop anywhere, just in case she was seen and someone casually mentioned to Peter that his wife had been out and about on Sunday night and wondering what she had been doing. She didn't want any unwanted spotlight falling on her behaviour. She needed to be able to keep an eye on her husband, unobserved and without raising any suspicions.

As she drove, she felt cold and not because the temperature was near freezing, but because of his actions. He was making her feel unloved, unwanted, cast aside. He had always been a little distant, it was his nature, but things had never been this bad. Their marriage had gradually cooled as the years went by, a bit like a soufflé deflating in slow motion. But what had really tested their relationship, was the issue of children.

The fact that she couldn't get pregnant, he treated as her failure, which in a way it was, at least physically speaking. But she'd not done anything to cause it. She'd not had some awful sexual disease that had rendered her barren. It seems she was just made that way. Her reproductive organs were flawed and that's precisely how he made her feel with his attitude. Instead of helping her through that terrible news by listening to her outpouring of emotion, he'd refused to discuss the subject. He'd said there was no need to talk about it. There was nothing to be done to rectify the situation. That was the end of the matter, as far as he was concerned.

She'd suggested adoption, but he'd said no for he wanted his child and no one else's. She'd proposed a surrogate. At that idea he'd looked at her as though she were mad, which perhaps she was, slightly, by then. However, she soon learned not to talk about it, not to bring the subject up. Learned to never mention babies, for when she did, he would turn on the television, pick up a book, or even walk out of the room. And so, gradually, it became something they never discussed. It was a subject never even thought about. But it was there, all the same, between them. Keeping them apart like an invisible wall, or the dome in Stephen King's novel. She was inside the dome and Peter was on the outside.

She parked her car back in its usual spot on the driveway and walked into the house. As she looked around their new quarter with fresh eyes, she saw what a lovely home she had. As an army wife, as Peter's wife, she had everything she could wish for; a good looking husband; a lovely house; a social life. She had friends; well she had the other wives on the garrison. There was always someone to talk to in a general sense, but no one she could tell her hopes and fears to. There was no one she could confide in, no best friend.

She went to close the curtains in the living room, glancing out at the dark quiet night. Out there, outside of this marriage, she would be alone, penniless, homeless. The thought made her shiver with fear and she let the curtains fall closed against the night. No, she had to make the best of things. To do that, their marriage must be allowed to get back on the right track. Peter needed to see her with new eyes and he couldn't do that while they were blinkered, while she was hidden from him by the cheap wiles of his latest whore.

Now she understood what Matilda had gone through. Matilda had said that those who'd abused her couldn't be allowed to get away with it. They had to pay and it was the same for Louise. The prostitutes couldn't be allowed to get away with taking her husband from her. They had to pay. And pay they would.

Twenty Three

I knew I had to get out of the house, but I was still too ashamed to go out in daylight. Too afraid of the reactions I would provoke. My solution was to walk the streets at night. That way my disfigurement could not be easily seen and if anyone did see my face, then it would be too dark for me to see the reaction in their eyes. To see the horror, the pity, the questioning looks. Whatever people thought, I didn't want them to see me and I didn't want to see them.

Sauntering past the school one evening, his school, I saw a notice calling a Governor's Meeting. It was to be held in two days' time. Dampening down my exuberance that I'd found a way to get the Headmaster on his own so easily, I hurried home to make my plans.

The school was on a fenced plot. But I knew the pedestrian access wasn't locked when the school was in use. It was only the entrance to the building itself that was locked. Hedging grew all along the perimeter fence and also along the path to the main entrance. Either would give me enough cover while I waited. The meeting would be held in the hall, or in the staff room. Both rooms were good for me as both were away from the main entrance. I thought about breaking in, perhaps through one of the classrooms and waiting inside the school for the meeting to break up. Waiting for everyone to go and leave him on his own. I was sure that would happen, for he would have to lock up once every one else had left the building. But I decided it wasn't worth the risk. There could be alarms that might go off and alert them to my presence.

So my plan was to wait in the shadows, outside the main door, which he would have to lock behind him and maybe even key in an alarm code. I didn't need long. I just wanted to have the opportunity to surprise him, while he was concentrating on the task of making his school secure overnight.

I was very agitated during the two day wait, unable to settle to even the simplest of tasks. The more I thought about my plan, the more I relived the awful things he had done to me. Reminders of my time with him came in wisps of memory, planting cobwebs of fear that I couldn't break free from, sticky skeins of silk that I couldn't get rid of.

At last the days passed and the evening I had waited so long for was upon me. It was a damp, dark night which I saw as a good omen. Low clouds covered the moon and people I passed were huddled in coats or hidden under umbrellas. No one took any notice of a woman hurrying down the street with her coat collar turned up, shielding her face as though to keep it out of the rain.

I slipped through the gate and was relieved to find the lights still on inside the school. Bars of yellow illuminated the playground, spilling out of the windows. I decided to risk a peek and saw several people sitting around tables that had been pulled together to make a large rectangle. As I watched, they began to stand, pushing back chairs that scraped along the floor and collecting bags, notebooks and briefcases. My teeth were on edge with the horrible screeching sound their chairs made. I quickly moved back to the corner of the building, next to the main entrance and waited in the shadows.

As I watched the governors leave, I ran my hand over the shard of glass I had in my pocket. It's cold hard surface focusing my mind and my hatred. And then it was time. The lights went out, one by one, until only the light above the door was still on. The bang of the main door echoed across the empty playground as he closed it behind him and I heard the jingle of keys in his hand.

I emerged from the bushes and with the element of surprise, I managed to push him hard against the door and pin him there. Grabbing a handful of hair from the back of his head, I slammed his forehead into the glass door, which stunned him. I turned his head to one side, so his ear was facing me. Into that orifice, which had heard my cries more times than I cared to remember, I plunged my long pointed shard of glass. It went through his eardrum, into his brain. I hoped the screams of his victims would accompany him on his journey to Hell, for surely no one as evil as he would ever be allowed into Heaven.

Twenty Four

Staff Sgt Jones' head was as bald as ever. Crane had often wondered if he shaved it every day, but now was more inclined to think that the man was just bald. He had never seen Jones' head with a five o'clock shadow on it. Crane found Jones in the middle of Provost Barracks, surrounded by his military policemen at shift change for the patrols. He stood for a moment watching as Jones issued the orders of the day and then dismissed his men who hurried out of the room, eager to take up their duties. The things that differentiated military personnel from civilians, Crane thought, were the mind-set, the willingness, the endeavour, the enjoyment. Being in the military was a lifestyle choice as much as a career choice. He knew some people would shoot him down, talk about entrepreneurs, businessmen and salesmen. Say that there were plenty of civilians around who were hard working and enjoyed their jobs. But Crane always felt that the forces were the only place you would find such loyalty and devotion in so many people. So much camaraderie that it was like one big family.

As Jones walked over, the two men decided to have

a smoke and talk outside, Jones bringing with him a slim file.

'I take it you've something for me then?' Crane said after lighting up and indicating the file.

'Yes, the file's a bit thin, I'm afraid. There are quite a few lads who have just come back from Germany as the RLC have just redeployed. But only a handful of soldiers brought cars back with them and they were mostly officers.'

'Ah,' said Crane.

'Ah, indeed,' said Jones.

Dealing with officers was not Crane's favourite occupation. Being an investigator in the Special Investigations Branch of the Military Police meant that Crane could cut across the chain of command. He could interview who he wanted, when he wanted and where he wanted. He could walk into the Officers' Mess if on investigation, if he wanted to. For the rank system meant nothing to the SIB. Most soldiers hated the Military Police and it seemed to follow that most officers hated the SIB. But Crane's motto was that it didn't matter what rank a man was, if he was guilty of a crime, then that was all that mattered.

Crane took the file and flipped it open. 'Any of these blokes known to you?' he asked Jones.

'No. They're all as clean as a whistle. Not even a couple of days in the guard house for fighting.'

The military police could detain soldiers for a few nights' detention for minor offences around the camp, or in town. There used to be a large military prison on Aldershot Garrison, built in the 1870's and modelled on Victorian civil prisons, such as Wormwood Scrubs. It was called 'The Glasshouse' due to its large glass lantern roof and was in use up until 1946 when it was destroyed by fire, during a riot. The term 'Glasshouse' came to mean any prison on any garrison, but the term had its origins in Aldershot, although it had faded from use. The only surviving military prison for the British Army was at Colchester.

'Alright,' said Crane. 'Thanks for this. I'll have to look through the info and see if any of their cars are a likely fit, although a dark mid-sized car isn't much to go on.'

Jones laughed. 'Is that what you're looking for?'

'Mmm,' said Crane putting out his cigarette. 'Why?'

'Because most of the cars brought back were brightly coloured Japanese sports cars.'

'You're kidding me?'

'Nope. Latest craze apparently, as they're much cheaper in Germany because of the exchange rate.'

'Bugger.' Crane thought for a moment, his hand itching to go to his packet of cigarettes and light up another one. But he resisted the temptation, trying as he was to cut down on his consumption. 'You said most?'

'Yes, but you're not going to like it.'

'Come on, Jones, spit it out.'

'In that case, the only likely suspect is the Colonel.'

'I beg your pardon? Did you just say the Colonel?'

'Yup. Brought back the wife's black Mercedes A7. You know the small hatchback type. Anyway it's already been re-plated with a UK number. The details are all in there. But that can't possibly be the one you're looking for, surely?'

Crane looked at Jones. Then down at the file. Then back to Jones and promptly walked away, heading for his car, leaving Jones to stare after him.

As Crane sat in his Ford Focus, he opened the file, checked an address, lit a cigarette, thought for a few moments and then came to a decision. He couldn't even begin to comprehend that Colonel Marshall had anything to do with the death of a prostitute. But Crane wouldn't be much of an investigator if he didn't follow up a lead. Not wanting to make a fool of himself, yet torn by the need to see the A7, Crane thought he'd do a drive past.

Starting the car, he drove off towards North Camp at the top of the Garrison, until he came to the Colonel's house. It was a throwback to an era when Aldershot was a larger Garrison, worthy of the title, 'The Home of the British Army'. It was a red bricked Victorian pile, the type of house his wife Tina loved. Crane preferred new himself and was quite happy with the modern three bed detached house they were quartered in whilst their own Victorian era semi was rented out. Tina had fought to stay in their own house, off the Garrison, but the birth of their first child Daniel, meant they just couldn't afford to live there whilst Tina wasn't working. So simple economics had made them rent out their own house and move to an army quarter. It suited Crane as he was closer to work and could be at the scene of an incident within minutes, but juxtaposed with that was the feeling that he never seemed to get away from work or the army. But then again he'd signed up for the lifestyle as much as the job, he reasoned to himself many times.

As Crane drove past Colonel Marshall's house he saw that, unusually for a garrison property, the Colonel's home was protected by hedgerow and had gates across the drive, with a large garden contained inside them. Turning around at the top of the street, Crane drove back, parked the car, got out and strolled past the open gate. There was only one car parked outside the house. A small, black, Mercedes A7. Crane stopped, taking out his cigarettes and lighter as an excuse to linger by the gate. He looked at the car for a few moments. The bodywork was unmarked and gleaming, at least from the back. Dropping his lighter, Crane squatted down to retrieve it, looking at the underneath of the car as he did so. The tyres were clean and as new and there didn't appear to be a trace of mud on them.

Twenty Five

Louise shivered as she finished reading the latest chapter in Matilda's story. How sad it was that the men, who had taken advantage of her, were the ones who should have been protecting her. First a man of God and then a school teacher, both the type of men regarded by society as being above reproach. But instead of being beacons of light in a young child's life, Matilda had revealed them as being no better than spiders or scorpions. Poisonous insects she had crushed underfoot and banished from the face of the earth.

As Louise moved about the house, after putting away Matilda's book, she realised that, of course, her case was similar. Peter was being tempted by the dregs of humanity, she recognised as she stacked the dishwasher, after rinsing the leftovers off the plates. Girls who had no pride and no self-esteem. Who were slaves to their pimps and their drug habit. She moved upstairs to make the bed, thinking of the whores. The worthless females who couldn't find normal jobs, who were fit for nothing, banished from normal society. She shook out the duvet and pummelled the pillows into submission, taking out her anger over the prostitutes

Peter was dallying with on her bedding.

Flinging open the curtains, she let light into the room and sunbeams crisscrossed the carpet like some sort of giant grid for playing noughts and crosses. Opening up the window, she leaned out, breathing in the crisp air, thinking of the girls who were forced to live their lives holed up in squalid rooms during the day, only coming out at night like vampires. She paced the bedroom, her anger building at the vampires of Aldershot. The girls who fed on the sexual impulses and urges of their victims. Taking advantage of the weakness of men.

Determined to help Peter, she realised she had to find his latest floosy. She had to find the girl in the black wig. Her husband needed saving from himself. He needed saving from his latest whore. He was going to be away this week end, just a short two day conference, but it meant he'd be away on Saturday night. That's when she would have her chance.

Getting ready to go to meet some of the wives for morning coffee, Louise reflected that over the past week she had been slightly happier. Peter had seemed less distant and as a result there had been fewer opportunities for that casual cruelty of his. The forgotten kisses, the forgotten goodbyes, his lack of attention when listening to her conversation. Those little things that stabbed at her, each one tiny in itself, but put them together...

Pushing her mind away from Peter's flaws as she brushed out her hair, she fancied he was being kinder out of guilt. Guilty because he'd had sex with another prostitute and still hadn't made love to his wife.

Louise ran down the stairs, checking her reflection in the lovely old mirror hanging on the hall wall. She was glad they'd kept it, kept something of the old house which they'd filled with their new. It was a tie to the history of the place, a reminder of past times, a reminder of Matilda her secret friend. She smiled to herself and gave a little wave goodbye to Matilda, then collected her car keys and slammed the door behind her on her way out. As she drove away, pausing at the gates to check the road was clear, she noticed a man on the pavement, smoking a cigarette. She hoped he wouldn't throw the butt into her garden.

It seemed the officer's wives weren't above a bit of gossip. Louise had joined them that morning wanting to talk about a local school that needed help with raising funds and were also in need of two school governors. As it was where most of the army children went, Louise was keen to make her mark on Aldershot Garrison with some positive, easily achieved results. She was happy to take one of the governor places if she could find someone to take the other. But her efforts to turn the conversation to the school were in vain. All the women wanted to talk about was the murder of the local prostitute.

'Who'd have thought Aldershot would have a red light area,' said one, who Louise thought was called Juliet.

'I thought most towns had them,' replied another. Louise didn't know this woman, still not having managed to meet everyone yet.

'Really? It's not something I've come across myself.' Juliet's comment caused tittering laughter, making her blush prettily. 'Still, murder's pretty awful. It doesn't matter who was killed.' Juliet had recovered her composure and was clearly trying to move the conversation away from the dead girl's occupation.

But the problem now was Louise's equanimity. She could feel a hot flush rising up, spreading from her chest, up her neck and by now she was convinced her cheeks must be a flaming red.

Juliet noticed her distress. 'Louise, are you alright?' she asked.

Everyone stopped talking and looked at her. Louise grabbed her notebook and waved it in front of her face like a fan, trying desperately to cool down, but the scrutiny from the ladies was making it worse.

'Um, yes,' Louise rapidly fanned the notebook. 'Sorry, bit of a hot flush.'

'Oh, you poor thing,' Juliet said. 'I know just how you feel,' and so began another topic of conversation, this time about the menopause.

Louise stumbled into the kitchen after mumbling about the need for a glass of water and drank it greedily, holding onto the sink for dear life.

Twenty Six

Lindsay moved around her bed-sitting room over the Unicorn pub in Aldershot. Her room was next to Sally's, who wasn't there anymore, of course. The yellow police tape across her friend's door reminding Lindsay every time she went out, or came in, of Sally's fate. She sniffed back a few tears at the thought. She really missed her. Missed the laughs, the giggles, telling raucous tales of the punters and keeping each other's spirits up when the reality of their profession hit them squarely in the face. Like a punter's fist. Sally had been given a black eye once from some idiot. Every time she saw him again after that she'd told him to fuck off or she'd knee him in the balls. Lindsay smiled at the memory. Sally had certainly had a way with her.

It wasn't fair. Sally had only been 19. She'd had all her life in front of her. She'd always said that one day she'd find someone nice. Someone who'd take her away from the sordid work they did. Away from the sex, the pawing, the hot breath, the sweaty smells. But Lindsay knew it was just a pipe dream. There were no knights on white horses to charge up and rescue them. Not in Aldershot at any rate, nor anywhere else for that matter.

Lindsay wiped away a tear and sat down on her bed, the old springs creaking in protest. She fancied the landlord deliberately put noisy beds in the rooms, to dissuade the girls from bringing anyone back. Bouncing, squeaking springs brought a cacophony of shouts, bangs and swearing from the other residents. All the rooms had the noisy beds. The landlord had probably bought them as a job lot.

Lindsay put on the clothes she'd laid out on the bed, jeans, sweater, boots, normal, sensible clothes. Dressed like that and without the harsh make up and black wig she wore when working, no one would have any inkling about her night job. She caught sight of herself in the large mirror she had propped up against one wall. There, definitely normal. She brushed her blond hair and then tied it up, pulling on a baseball cap and pushing her hair through the gap at the back.

Turning to grab her bag from the chair, she saw her books and papers laid out on a small table she used as a desk. She hadn't had a good education when she was growing up, because of being moved around from children's home to children's home or foster parents to foster parents. The nomadic life in care meaning she bibbed and bobbed from school to school. Where she was always the new girl, never really fitting in. Because of her lack of qualifications, she'd found it difficult to find a job. She was no good at office work and hated being confined all day in bland offices with bland people. Shops were just as bad in their own way. It was tempting to pilfer bits and pieces. Nothing fancy or expensive, just chocolate, lipstick or soap. But she'd been caught and was 'let go' as they'd put it. So she had no choice but to turn to the oldest profession. At least spreading her legs gave her time to study during the day. She was trying to get some qualifications, for she really did want to better herself. She was in a horrible profession, but not stuck in it. Prostitution was just a bus stop on life's journey. At least she didn't have a pimp to pay like some of the other girls, or was addicted to drink or drugs.

Reaching out her hand to open her door, she saw her black wig hanging from a hook on the back of it. Lindsay liked to wear a wig when she was working as it changed her into someone else. It was a mask, a disguise, the other side of her personality in a way. It was an act, a way of separating herself from the work she did. Whoring was, for her, just a way to make money.

Slamming the door behind her and locking it, Lindsay made her way out of the pub and onto the street. She was going to meet Diane Chambers from the Aldershot News, to give an interview about her friend Sally. She had to do anything she could to help find Sally's killer and had been pleased that Diane had seemed eager to interview her, when Louise had telephoned the newspaper. The killer, whoever he was, couldn't be allowed to get away with it. The police had to catch him. They just had to.

Twenty Seven

At last it was Saturday night. Peter had left early that morning and Louise had hugged her secret to herself as she waved him goodbye. By the time he came home on Sunday, all his problems would be solved. Rather fancying herself as his saviour, Louise turned her attention to the matter in hand. She was plagued by questions. Would the girl be working? What lure could she use to get her away? Would the lesbian angle work again? Occasionally she'd had doubts. Could she do it again? Should she do it again? But those thoughts were erased by conjuring up a picture of Peter in her mind. His proud military bearing couldn't be tarnished by these girls. He couldn't lose the one thing he loved. The army. And so once again her resolve hardened.

Louise had been unable to eat all day, because of the tension and as a result by mid-evening she was becoming giddy and lightheaded. Deciding she needed to eat, even though the thought filled her with repulsion and her stomach rolled in protest, she fancied she could eat some chicken. And so a plan was formulated. Firstly she would go and get something to eat, and then see if she could find the girl in the black wig.

Louise ran upstairs to get ready. She dressed in the dark clothing that she had selected earlier, made sure she had a new pair of leather gloves with her and then went to get her beautiful shard of glass. She ran down to the basement and kneeling on the dusty floor, opened the flaps of the cardboard box which contained the broken pieces of the mirror from her bedroom. Pulling on her gloves, she inspected the shards; selecting one that she was satisfied had a point which was sharp enough and was long and thin enough. The glass reflected parts of the basement as she examined it, giving her glimpses of the chest and the white silk scarf within. Louise's heart was filled with a sudden surge of emotion, making her blink back tears. It was Matilda's presence, of course. Her one and only friend hadn't abandoned her in her hour of need. Louise felt herself being filled with the spirit of Matilda. Her friend gave her courage, hope and resolve. Wrapping the glass carefully in a towel she silently thanked Matilda for being her inspiration, for showing her how she could save her marriage. As she left the basement, she knew Matilda would be with her every step of the way.

The local Kentucky Fried Chicken was in the High Street, which was pedestrian only, so Louise manoeuvred her A7 around the back streets, eventually pulling up next to the loading bays behind the take-away. As she parked and turned off the car engine, she glanced up. From where she was parked, she could see the side of the fast food outlet. A girl pushed her way out of the door. High heels, short skirt, breasts on display and, could it be possible, black, sharply cut, bobbed hair. The girl walked towards Louise, stuffing chips into her mouth as she moved away from the bright lights of the High Street and into the shadows of the alley. Louise was surprised, yet grateful. She supposed that even whores needed to eat. This would save her a great deal of anxiety, not to mention time.

Louise climbed out of the car, crossed the road and walked up the alley towards the prostitute, her footsteps echoing around the passage, like a harbinger of doom. But the whore was oblivious to the footsteps and to Louise. She was focused on her meal, her head bent towards the cardboard box in her hand. There was no one else around just Louise and the whore. This was an unbelievable co-incidence. It was now or never. Louise had to grab the opportunity that had presented itself. Taking a shuddering breath, she felt the power of the shard of glass in her hand and stepped forward to stand in the girl's path.

Looking at her watch, Louise tapped it. A puzzled look crossed her face and she said to the girl, 'Have you got the right time, please? My watch seems to have stopped.'

The whore looked up from her meal and Louise saw her face and hair close up and was convinced she had found the right one. This was the prostitute that had ensnared her husband.

'What?' the girl mumbled through a mouth full of chips.

Dear God, thought Louise, the girl can't even reply to a civil question.

'What's the time, please?'

'Don't know,' and the girl returned to her meal, picking up a piece of chicken.

Without any warning, Louise turned slightly and slammed her body into the whore, who fell backwards in shock and hit the floor with a thump. The chicken flew out of her hand and her chips were scattered across the tarmac.

Without thinking Louise sat on the girl's chest, punching the air out of her lungs. She grabbed her face, jerked it to the side and ground her cheek into the pavement.

'This will teach you to fuck my husband,' she hissed into the whore's unprotected ear, before plunging her shard of glass deep inside it.

As the light went out of the girl's eyes, to be replaced by a death stare, Louise sighed in satisfaction. Then in one smooth movement, Louise pushed herself of the girl's now lifeless body, brushed dirt and chips off her coat and returned to the A7. The incident had happened so quickly that only a couple of minutes had passed. Louise started the car and drove away, all thoughts of buying some chicken forgotten.

Twenty Eight

When Crane arrived on the scene of the murder of a second girl, the police forensic team were shooing away the cats that were trying to get to the fast food littered around the body. The lure of chicken was strong though and Crane watched as the cats slunk off and hid in the shadows of the alley, loath to abandon the unexpected meal. The occasional glint of green eyes could still be seen, watching Crane as he walked up the passageway.

While the tent was put in place over the girl's body, Crane and Anderson climbed into protective gear, wanting a quick look before the team began their painstaking and time consuming work. As soon as it was ready, Anderson walked over to the tent, pulled back the flap, calling for Crane to join him.

They walked silently into the tent that was lit by large outdoor lights hung from the framework. They police had managed to get a power source from KFC and cables snaked down the alley from the shop and into the tent. It saved a lot of noise from a generator and Crane and Anderson could hear each other for once. Well they could have done, if they were speaking.

For all either of them could seem to do was to stare at the girl on the floor. A dead girl with a black bobbed hairdo and a shard of glass sticking out of her ear.

'Lindsay,' Anderson broke the silence and spoke first.

'Shit,' replied Crane as he squatted down by Lindsay's head. 'On initial examination, it seems to be the same glass, or at least very similar to the one from Sally's murder. It looks like it's from a mirror again at any rate.'

Crane looked at the small dribble of blood trailing out of Lindsay's ear, a pathetic trickle from such a fatal blow. He wasn't looking forward to Major Martin's explanation on this death. There would no doubt be more brains and goo on this piece of glass also. The odour of fried chicken and chips from the KFC kitchen was trapped inside the plastic tent and Crane was sure he'd never buy another meal from them. Their food being forever linked in his mind to Lindsay's death.

Retiring from the tent, so the forensic team and photographer could get to work, Crane and Anderson pulled off their white suits and wandered away from the clutch of spectators that had lined up against the police tape at the entrance to the alleyway.

Anderson's phone rang, and he answered it, listening briefly before cutting the call and replacing the mobile in his pocket. 'Any thoughts?' he asked Crane.

'The murderer could be a man who hates whores, sees them as nothing more than trash to be disposed of. He could hate women in general and sees these girls as easy pickings, I suppose.'

'But why kill her here and not down on the industrial estate?' Anderson said.

'A chance meeting? A twist of fate? And why

Lindsay?' Crane asked more questions as he patted his pockets trying to find his cigarettes and lighter.

'Because she made a fuss about Sally's murder, maybe?'

'Or saw something she shouldn't have?'

'And didn't realise its significance,' Anderson finished their most unsatisfactory train of thought.

'Anyway, why am I here?' Crane asked, at last finding his cancer sticks and lighting up.

'I thought it would interest you.'

'Really? Haven't I seen enough murder scenes in my career?'

'Come on, Crane. There are two reasons you are here. One is that it is the same MO as last time. The second is that I got onto the CCTV centre at Farnborough as soon as I heard about the murder. That was them on the phone. They've found something interesting already. A small dark hatchback was spotted driving around the area, with foreign licence plates on, although they haven't yet been able to identify the number. So, have you had any luck tracking down any soldiers returning from Germany with such a car?'

'Not really,' Crane stalled. 'It's more common than you'd think. What am I supposed to do? Check every dark hatchback owned by every soldier on a garrison of thousands of men?'

'Yes,' Anderson said. 'That's precisely what you need to do.'

Crane turned and stomped away. Fuck. He'd nearly said Mercedes A7 instead of dark hatchback. He didn't like withholding information from Anderson. Their friendship went too far back and they worked too closely for Crane to keep vital facts from him for very long. But his loyalty to the Army was stronger.

Twenty Nine

Doesn't anyone care?
Editorial Comment by Diane Chambers
Chief Crime Reporter, Aldershot News

That was the question asked by a young woman, Lindsay Hatton, when I interviewed her about the murder of her friend Sally Smith. And now Lindsay is also dead, no doubt by the same hand. Murdered by the vengeful killer who is stalking young prostitutes innocently plying their wares in Aldershot.

And so I ask again, doesn't anyone care?

Two young girls are dead. The police have no leads, no forensic evidence and no idea who the killer is. At least that is the impression they are giving, with their regular spouting of, 'no comment' or 'the investigation is continuing' babble. Which can only mean one thing. They have no idea what is going on, or who the killer is.

I recently interviewed Lindsay for a poignant piece about her background and listened to her pleas for help in finding Sally's killer. And now Lindsay is dead also. It's a tragedy.

But they were only whores, I hear some of you say.

In reply, I would urge you to read the interview next to this editorial piece. Sally and Lindsay were ordinary girls, who just happened to take what some of you may consider to be the wrong turning in life. They could have been your daughter, your sister, your niece, your cousin. Don't let their profession colour your view of them. Don't judge them. Help them. Show that their deaths have not been in vain. If anyone has any information at all that can help the police catch this brutal killer or killers, I and my newspaper, urge you to come forward.

I personally promise to help the police as much as I can. I will carry on Lindsay's work and try and find her killer. Was it Lindsay's investigation of her friend's death that put her in jeopardy? Did asking questions put her in the killer's sights? Are any of the night girls safe?

I care.

The Aldershot News cares.

Now it's your turn to show the police that the good people of Aldershot care.

If you know anything, or have seen anything, please pass on the information. The murder team can be contacted via Crimestoppers on 0800 555 111 or call the officer in charge of the investigation, D I Anderson directly at Aldershot Police station.

Crane threw the newspaper down on his desk. It was the third time he'd read the article. Bloody Diane Chambers. As always, her article was high on rhetoric and low on fact. He was only glad that she hadn't mentioned the army's involvement for once. Perhaps that was Billy's influence. He certainly hoped so. He knew that Diane had a point, though. Prostitution was not usually high on people's wish list of professions to aspire to. Nor did whores seem to be on the radar when crimes were committed against them. Most people just didn't see them or think about them at all. Out of sight, out of mind, he supposed.

He jumped at the sound of his telephone ringing and when he answered it, found DI Anderson on the line, or at least he thought it was Anderson. He couldn't really hear him.

'Derek?' asked Crane. 'Is that you?' he shouted over the background noise of ringing telephones, shouting and banging of doors.

'Of course it's bloody me,' he heard. Then a door slammed and the background noises faded away and Crane could hear him properly. 'Jesus Christ. Have you seen this morning's local paper?' Derek snapped in Crane's ear.

'Just read it. Why?' Crane couldn't help the smile that was forming, for he could guess what was coming.

'Because it's gone bloody nuts here. The phones haven't stopped ringing and there's a queue running all along the outside wall of the police station of people waiting to see me. I'll ring that bloody woman's neck when I next see her. She named me as the officer in charge of the case. In print.'

By now, Crane was openly chuckling. 'So it seems that the mighty people of Aldershot have heeded Diane's call to arms then.'

'Fucking idiots,' Anderson grumbled. 'Oh and you might like to turn your television on.'

'Why?'

'Because there's now a candlelit vigil outside the KFC on the High Street. People are streaming there, placing flowers, candles, teddy bears, bloody all sorts.'

'That's nice,' said Crane.

'Nice? It might be nice but it's giving me the biggest manpower headache I've ever had. I've had to cancel leave, pull in people to work early and make them stay late, just to man the phones in the station and to control the crowd outside the KFC.'

'I bet KFC will make a few bob out of this,' Crane said, deliberately being provocative.

'They would do, if the mourners weren't in the way and if they'd stop putting flowers in the open doorway. The manager is going nuts. They're driving away customers with all the weeping and wailing. And apparently someone is handing out hymn books as they're waiting for the local church choir to arrive to lead them in a sing song.'

'Our good citizens aren't doing things by halves then?' Crane was desperately trying to suppress his laughter, without much success.

'Don't you bloody laugh, Crane, or I'll come over there myself and strangle you.'

'Now, now, Derek, calm down. Look, the good people of Aldershot do seem to be going over the top on this one, I'll grant you that. I suspect most of them just want to get on the telly. The old 'five minutes of fame' syndrome. Do you want Jones to send down some MPs to help you out? They could control the crowds outside KFC.'

'Don't you dare!' roared Anderson. 'Diane Chambers would go around telling everyone that there's Marshall Law on the streets of Aldershot. She'd create a riot.'

'So she would. Oh well, you can't say I didn't try to help.'

'Of course you can help. Get Jones to send some military police boys down to the station, dressed in civvies. They can help answer these bloody phones and interview some people for me.'

Crane went to say that of course he would, but Anderson had already gone. After one last irreverent laugh he composed his face and went to find Jones. It wasn't that he didn't care. Crane and Anderson were the two who cared the most, Crane suspected. It was just that you had to love the people of Aldershot. There were two reactions from them. One: to do absolutely nothing. Or two: to go way, way, over the top. There was never an in-between.

Thirty

After sorting out some help for Derek with Staff Sgt Jones, Crane had a meeting with Captain Draper. He found the boss relaxing in his office, slurping what appeared to be a freshly made mug of coffee. Unfortunately Draper didn't offer Crane any, but he was invited to sit down. Draper's salt and pepper hair appeared to be freshly cut and his normal inscrutable face crinkled into a smile as Crane sat in front of him. Draper had been a senior non-commissioned officer in the military police, before taking a commission. The two men got on well because of this background, Crane being more receptive to a boss who had come up through the ranks, rather than some inexperienced captain straight out of the Officer Training College at Sandhurst.

Crane handed his boss a hard copy of the investigation file, which Draper didn't open, merely putting it down on his empty desk.

'You can tell me what's in the file,' he said and so Crane began by outlining the salient facts of the case to his boss. Two prostitutes had been killed, one in the middle of no-where and one outside the KFC in

Aldershot High Street. Public appeals had been made for information and as the Aldershot Police were somewhat inundated with calls and visits from the public, Crane had complied with Anderson's request to send some military policemen to work alongside the civilian police. Draper nodded his agreement with the arrangement. Crane then went on to say that twice a small black hatchback sporting German plates had been seen in the vicinity of the murders. As a result DI Anderson was keen to find out about any army personnel moving back from a German base into the area and bringing with them a German plated car.

'Well, that all seems very straightforward to me, Crane,' said Draper relaxing back in his chair. 'I take it there's a 'but' though, otherwise you wouldn't be here.'

'Yes, boss, I'm just not sure how big of a 'but' it is. It's the dark hatchback type car that has been seen at both locations and sporting a German number plate on it, or at least a foreign one. The only car of that type that has been repatriated is a Mercedes A7.'

'And? Who does it belong to? Frankly, Crane, I'm not seeing your problem.'

'It, um, belongs to the Colonel Marshall, Royal Logistics Corp, recently returned from Gutersloh.'

Draper was in the middle of taking a large gulp of his coffee when Crane had spoken. Spluttering, he put down his mug and managed, 'Say again?'

So Crane did, watching the disbelief cross Draper's face, before his boss managed to force his features into something resembling a more normal expression.

'Okay,' Draper said, with the air of a man trying his best to calm down. 'Let's go over it again. A dark hatchback doesn't mean specifically a Mercedes A7. Also that car has a UK number plate now, yes?'

'Yes and I've actually seen the car, sir. It was very clean and sporting a UK plate.'

'And it belongs to the Colonel's wife?'

'Yes, sir, and we've confirmed that with DVLA. It's in her name.'

'But there's no evidence to prove it's the car Anderson is looking for.'

'No, boss, nothing irrefutable at any rate.'

'Well, that's good then,' Draper looked relieved. 'The Colonel and his wife are surely beyond reproof. Let's face it, how would the man get to be a Colonel if there was a murderous side to him?' Draper grabbed the file and handed it back to Crane. 'No, Crane, I think you must be wrong on this one. Decision made. The Colonel's car is nothing to do with the investigation.'

'But,' Crane got no further.

'And you can take that as an order, Sgt Major,' Draper intervened.

'Sir,' Crane acknowledged Draper's decision.'

'I'm sure there are actual military cases that you should be concentrating on.'

'Certainly, sir,' Crane replied and left Draper's office.

But Crane wasn't as relieved as he thought he would be. He still had that niggling doubt somewhere in the back of his mind. It was about time he tried to find out where the Colonel had been on the nights in question. But it needed to be done subtly and Crane wasn't known for his subtlety.

Thirty One

Louise was at a loose end and had gone into Farnborough to look for some new clothes, but so far hadn't seen anything she liked. As a result, she made up her mind to go to Reading later in the week, where there was a much better selection of shops in the large shopping centre, the Oracle. Peter had one of those 'do's' coming up that they were expected to attend as a couple and she wanted something new to wear. A little black dress she supposed, but perhaps something a little more daring than she normally wore, something a little sexier without being overt. Peter would expect her to dress with decorum, but surely that didn't mean dowdy? She was beginning to feel her dress sense was rather too old fashioned after meeting the wives on Aldershot garrison. Her and Peter had obviously spent far too many years in Germany, Louise decided and as a result she was way behind in the current fashions.

Deep in thought, Louise nearly collided with a pram. 'Oh, sorry,' she exclaimed as she grabbed onto it, to stop herself falling. 'I must have been miles away,' she explained to the mother who seemed equally as shocked that someone had just grabbed her baby's buggy.

Unfortunately Louise glimpsed the baby as she straightened. She froze on the spot, remaining hunched over the pram like some hulking ogre. But if she were the beast, then the child was the picture of beauty. Louise could see blond wavy hair, long lashes and a little pink mouth.

'Oh, how gorgeous,' said Louise, the words escaping before she could stop them.

'Thanks,' said the young mum casually, as though everyone said that to her about her baby. Which they probably did, Louise realised and wondered if the young woman knew how lucky she was. The woman was talking to her, or at least Louise thought she was, as she could see the girl's lips moving. But she could hear nothing. Nodding, because she felt she ought to do something, Louise then stumbled away, wanting to get as far from the baby as possible.

Her flight was stopped by the plate glass window of a store. Louise looked up and saw she had bumped into the window of Mothercare. As she looked inside, she saw the store was filled with pregnant women, mothers with children and older women with and without grandchildren in tow. Gaily printed little clothes were everywhere, racks upon racks of them. And then there were the cots, buggies, blankets, soft toys and accessories. Louise spun away from the window but everywhere she looked along the length of the shopping centre were more babies. They were cooing, gurgling, being fed, being played with. She was surrounded by them. She had to get out of the shopping centre, but they blocked her exit. She felt as fearful as if she were in an Alfred Hitchcock movie, one which was full of babies instead of birds.

Louise sunk to the floor, still leaning against the

Mothercare window. Why couldn't she have a child? What had she done that was so very wrong, to be made to suffer like this? Round and round in her head went the conversation with the gynaecologist all those years ago.

'So sorry, Louise, but I'm afraid it's bad news...' the Doctor had started and then proceeded to tell her she'd never be able to have children. Never. Ever.

And where had Peter been when she'd needed him? Not with her at the hospital. Never with her. Always with his beloved army. And so she'd had to hear the news on her own without any support from him, as he'd not been able to get away from some important briefing or other. During heated, horrible arguments after that terrible news, he'd said he couldn't forgive her for being barren. But did he ever think that she couldn't forgive him for not being there in her hour of need?

Standing on legs that felt as wobbly as jelly, she pushed herself off the window and made her way unsteadily to the car, taking deep breaths as she walked and looking at the ground instead of around her.

The drive home, all of three miles, passed in a blur of automatic pilot and once there, she closed the front door and leaned against it. Tears of self-pity streamed down her face as she stood in the cold, empty house.

Which echoed how she felt. Cold. Empty.

In that moment of clarity Louise realised she had nothing and nobody. The only thing she had was the book. And the only person she had was Matilda. Retrieving the book from its hiding place, she curled up on the bed, still wearing her coat and greedily read the next entry....

Thirty Two

I had now dealt with the vicar and the headmaster. It was time to turn my attention to the next man on my list. I had to get him on his own. And it had to be somewhere where he wouldn't be found for a while. Also there may be people about, so I needed to do something about my appearance. All in all this killing called for more creativity and involved me going out in the day. Would I be able to do it? Walk outside those gates in broad daylight? My palms sweated at the thought. But I decided my desire to kill him overrode my fear and I picked up the telephone.

When his receptionist answered the phone, I asked for an appointment.

'I could give you 2pm, tomorrow.'

'Is there a later one available?' I asked. 'Only I don't want to take time off from work if at all possible,' I lied.

'Um, well I suppose I could give you the last appointment of the day. He will stay on if it's urgent. Is it? Urgent?'

'Oh, that would be so kind,' I gushed.

'Very well, 6pm tomorrow.'

We then went through the formalities of my name and brief description of my problem and she also gave me directions to the consulting rooms.

Replacing the telephone I smiled to myself. I'd done it. Now I had just over 24 hours to prepare myself and arrange transport as the address was in a nearby town and I wouldn't have a car that afternoon. After several phone calls it seemed the best way to get there would be by bus. But, of course, the initial journey at least would be in daylight. I toyed with the idea of buying a wig, to change my hair colour and to cover my face with long tresses. But that would involve going out also.

I wandered upstairs and into the attic. There were a number of hats there, I recalled, perhaps one of those would be suitable. Climbing the steep wooden stairs I opened the small door and stepped into my make-believe world. I'd put all the clothes, hats and scarves in one large chest. That was it! I remembered a scarf, plain white and silky and decided that could work. Scrabbling through the contents of the chest, I came to the item I wanted. Walking over to the mirror I placed the scarf over my head, crossed the ends under my chin and then wound them round my neck to tie at the back. Looking at myself this way and that in the mirror, I fiddled with the back until I was satisfied. The effect was very Audrey Hepburn. It transformed me from a scarred shadow of my former self, into a film star. It covered my hair, hid my scar and made me look sophisticated. All I needed now was a long cigarette holder, I giggled to myself. Then I repressed my laughter. This was no laughing matter. I had to concentrate, for I would soon be able to claim my third victim.

Thirty Three

When Peter returned home that night he found Louise watching the television. She raised a tear stained face to his.

'Oh, Peter, have you seen this?'

He wanted to snap at her to say that of course he'd not seen the television that day. He'd been working. But he swallowed his angry retort and said, 'No, why?'

'Another girl has been killed. And look, people are lighting candles, leaving flowers and trinkets for her.'

Peter glanced up, just in time to see a photograph of a girl with sharply cut black hair and red, red lips. He grabbed the back of Louise's chair to steady himself.

'Who's that?' he managed to ask.

'Oh, that's the girl who was killed. Look, there's another photo of her. That must be a friend with her. Doesn't she look different without all that stuff on her face?'

The girl's hair had been replaced by a blond ponytail and this time she wore very little make up. The news reporter said, 'These are two pictures of the same girl, Lindsay Hatton. In the first she is dressed for work and the second is a picture of her taken with her friend

Sally, who has also been killed. Sally's body was found recently, near woodland in Badshot Lea.'

The photos disappeared from the screen, to be replaced by images of people maintaining a vigil in Aldershot High Street. Peter was still holding onto the back of Louise's chair. His hand was clutching it so tight, that his knuckles were white. Both girls killed. Both girls that he had gone with. Someone appeared to be killing his prostitutes. With great effort, he prised his hands off the chair.

'I'm, um, just going to get changed,' he managed to say before turning away and running up the stairs.

Were the killings anything to do with him? They couldn't be surely. Did anyone know he had been picking up prostitutes? No, he didn't think so. Or at least he hoped not.

He stripped off his clothes and stepped into the shower. No so much because he was hot and sweaty, but because he wanted to slough the touch of Sally and Lindsay off his skin. Wash them all away so he could emerge clean and safe from his shower and no one would be any the wiser.

Once dry and dressed in sweat pants and tee-shirt he went downstairs. Following his nose, he found Louise in the kitchen, bending over boiling pans.

'Oh, hi,' she said, turning to him. 'Dinner will be ready shortly.'

'Okay, I'll go and fix us a drink.'

Returning to the sitting room, Peter was glad to see the television was turned off. But on the drinks cabinet was a copy of the Aldershot News. The bloody story was following him wherever he went in the house. He swiped at it and it fell to the floor, where he left it. Grabbing a bottle of wine and two glasses from the cabinet, he returned to the kitchen and sat there sipping his drink, watching Louise as she pottered around the kitchen.

'I see the story's in the paper,' he said after a few minutes silence.

'Oh yes, it's the biggest thing ever to happen in Aldershot, apparently.'

'And you know that how? We've only just arrived.'

'Oh, from the other wives. It's all anyone can talk about. They're saying it's so exciting to have a serial killer in Aldershot and everyone's wondering who it could be.'

Peter emptied his glass of wine in one large gulp as though it were beer instead of good red wine and poured himself another.

1976

Mark Harmon sat behind his desk and surveyed his private consulting room in a break between patients. He finished writing up the report on the woman he'd just seen, using his fountain pen full of bluc/black ink. He smoothed his silk tie out of the way as he wrote. He'd had an accident once and managed to get an ink stain on a particularly favourite tie. Since then he'd changed his pen and the Mont Blanc now took pride of place on his desk.

It was just one lesson learned in his transition from doctor in the National Health Service to consultant in the private sector. Who would have thought that a scandal would have turned out to be his salvation?

Finishing his notes, he looked at his watch. Nearly 6pm. He was just waiting for the last patient. He pulled towards him the notes from his secretary and cast his eye over the few details she'd taken over the phone. Yet another middle-aged woman with psychiatric problems. He was getting a bit tired of stale, older women, to be honest. That was the only thing wrong with psychiatry. There weren't enough pubescent girls needing help and guidance.

Which reminded him of his time in the NHS. A time when he'd had unfettered access to young girls. In his role as a general practitioner for various orphanages and children's charities, his work had allowed him to indulge his partiality for young flesh. But then that meddling social worker had stepped in. One child or other had objected to his close examination and the bloody woman had actually listened and then instead of turning away and doing nothing, she'd had the temerity to confront him. After some negotiation, she'd agreed not to tell the police if he left general practice and moved away. He had no choice but to agree as at least that way he wouldn't be struck off the Medical Register.

At the time he'd been alternately angry, fearful and desolate. He'd thought his life was over. But then his luck changed. It was as though he had a guardian angel looking out for him. An old friend from medical school, Stephen Baker, was looking for a psychiatrist to join him in private practice. Mark hadn't any money, but it hadn't mattered. Stephen's family were loaded and were bankrolling the practice. Mark had wondered about the fact that he hadn't specialised in psychiatry, but again Stephen over-ruled that objection, saying he'd much rather work with someone he knew, than someone he didn't.

And so gone was the white coat, the cheap suits, corduroy trousers and suede shoes, to be replaced by far better fitting pure wool ensembles. At £50 a throw, each consultation cemented the metamorphosis from under paid, over worked GP, to overpaid and underworked consultant. That was why he didn't mind staying late for one extra patient. The money. It was always about the money.

Mark glanced at the piece of paper again to check the name of the new client. Tilda Underwood. It didn't ring a bell. He'd never come across a Tilda before. It was an interesting name. The only connection he could think of was a child he'd once known called Matilda. His recollection of her innocent white skin, red hair and green eyes flooded into his brain, taking his breath away, the image as real as though she were standing in front of him. She had been a particular favourite. He'd invented several infections that had needed his close attention, just to keep her with him for as long as possible.

At a knock on his door, the picture of Matilda flew away and once again Mark was sitting in his office. But tendrils of the image persisted as his next patient entered the room.

Thirty Four

Crane had managed to keep away from Anderson and had told him by phone that despite lots of digging by Jones and himself, there were no cars around the garrison that were small and dark with German plates on. Which, of course, was the truth, as all the cars had been re-plated. It salved his conscience somewhat, as he wasn't really keeping anything from Anderson. Anyway he was following orders. It wasn't his decision or problem anymore. Wasn't it?

Then a few days after that conversation Anderson phoned, wanting Crane to look at CCTV film of someone in the vicinity of Lindsay's body, near to the rear of the KFC outlet around the time of the murder. Crane made his way to Aldershot Police Station somewhat reluctantly and not even the lure of Anderson's steady supply of cakes and biscuits helped brighten his mood.

The two men settled down in an interview room to view the footage, Anderson's office being too full of clutter and files to offer comfortable viewing. They looked at the footage together on Anderson's laptop. They watched a figure appear in the area of the camera, walk toward the alley leading to the shopping area and KFC and then disappear from view once more.

'Is this the only camera that caught her?' asked Crane.

'Yes, it's the only one within range. There's nothing in that alleyway and it seems she didn't go as far as the shopping area, or into the take-away itself. I've had people combing all the camera footage they can find, but with no luck. Our best guess is that this woman could be another prostitute, but we can't identify her,' said Anderson.

'Or she could just be a random person.'

'Woman.'

'Sorry?' said Crane.

'The figure is more than likely a woman. Look at the hair, it's long and curly.'

'Plenty of men have long curly hair.'

Anderson sighed in exasperation. 'Have you ever seen her before? Do you think she's a working girl?'

'Why? Do you think I use prostitutes? Are you insinuating there's something wrong with my marriage?' Crane knew he was biting, but couldn't seem to help it.

'Don't be stupid. I meant had you ever come across her during your investigation of other cases?'

'No sorry can't help,' said Crane. 'She doesn't look familiar at all. Anyway you can't see enough of her face; a bulky scarf around her neck covers most of it. She's just a slim woman with dark curly hair. How the hell am I supposed to recognise anyone from that?'

The only outstanding feature was the eyes, Crane felt. They were very striking almond shaped, cat-like eyes. But he kept that observation to himself and after finishing his cup of tea he left Anderson still frowning at the CCTV footage and returned to Provost Barracks.

Thirty Five

I managed to make it to Mark Harmon's office on time despite having to take the bus there. Not that I minded using public transport, or at least I hadn't before. Before the attack that is. With my headscarf on I was at least sparing my fellow passengers a glimpse of my ravaged face. Everyone told me that it didn't look that bad now. That my cheek had healed really well. But I didn't believe them. They didn't have to stare at the injury every day in the mirror. The livid raised scars on my pale skin seemed to pulse. They had a life of their own, as though an alien being had landed on the side of my face and was feeding on me.

Even though my hair and face were covered by the white headscarf, I felt unsteady as I walked through the streets, my eyes averted from the shop windows, cast down just in case anyone, or even I, inadvertently caught a glimpse of my face. I didn't want to see pity or more likely the revulsion in people's eyes.

I arrived at his consulting room a few minutes early and stood looking at the building. The doctor had rooms in an elegant old building of Georgian proportions. A discreet bronze plaque bore the engraved names of the two men inside. But it was only Mark Harmon who interested me, not the other man. I walked up the few steps to the front door and I traced his name with my finger, feeling a frisson of fear as I did so. But then anger pushed away my anxiety, as I thought about the acts he had inflicted on me, reinforcing the purpose of my visit. I pushed the bell and the door clicked open, sealing his fate.

The receptionist was waiting behind her desk in the hallway. 'Ah, Mrs Underwood,' she said after I'd introduced myself. 'The doctor is waiting for you. Please go through,' she pointed to a door. 'Doctor will see you out after your consultation, as I'll be gone by then.'

'Thank you,' I replied smoothly, trying to fall into the role of Audrey Hepburn and I knocked on his consulting room door.

As I sat in front of his large masculine desk, he took some initial details and then asked why I felt the need to see a psychiatrist.

'I want retribution, payback for what has been done to me,' I told him.

He looked surprised. Perhaps I'd been more vehement in my tone than I'd intended.

'What has been done to you?'

If he recognised me, he gave no sign. But then I suppose I was all grown up now. I pushed my headscarf off my head to expose my cheek, so he could see my disfigurement.

He gasped at the sight of my exposed face.

'This,' I said, not needing to point at the scarring.

'Oh my,' he managed to stammer.

'I think you should come closer and have a good look. I'm surprised that you don't recognise me. Have you forgotten me already, Dr Harmon? Surely not. For I've not forgotten you. I'm Matilda. I was once your very special friend. Or at least that's what you used to call me.'

He remained where he was, not seeming inclined to move. So I went to him. As I walked around his desk, he pressed backwards into his chair, becoming trapped up against the wall. For once he was the fearful one. For once he was the victim not the perpetrator. It was a delicious role reversal. It felt so right. Felt so good. But it seemed that Dr Harmon was so shocked by my presence and my words that he was frozen. Panic stricken. Perhaps he thought I was going to expose him. Tell the world about his guilty, dirty secrets. But exposure wasn't my game plan. Before he could react, I plunged the shard of glass into his neck.

'There,' I said, 'I told you I wanted retribution.'

As recognition flooded his eyes, his mouth opened and shut and his hands grabbed at his neck. So I pulled out the glass shard for him, as that was what he seemed to want me to do, allowing his blood to pump out of his body. Once he was still and quiet and the gurgling and choking noises had stopped, I left his office. As good as her word, his receptionist had gone home for the night. I was fairly certain his body wouldn't be found until the following morning.

Thirty Six

Louise dressed with more than a little trepidation that evening. Would Peter approve of her choice of dress? Would he think it too daring? Think it exposed too much flesh? The long black dress clung to her slim figure showing off her flat stomach that had not been stretched by pregnancy. Her breasts were still pert as they had never known the suckling of a child. The dress showed just a hint of cleavage and a slit at the front accentuated her long legs. She had left her hair down and it bounced on her shoulders, the red and brown colours catching the light, showing off the perfect highlights from her latest hairdresser. She had accentuated her green eyes with eyeliner and mascara, giving a look which spoke of promise and hidden depths. Twisting this way and that in the mirror in the bathroom, for they had still not replaced the broken one in the bedroom, Louise told herself to stop worrying. She liked the dress even if he didn't. She picked up her clutch bag, draped a shawl around her shoulders and strode to the bedroom door. And stopped. Hand in mid-air. Frozen.

All her bravado had faded away to nothing, as

though it were nothing more than a mirage.

But then she pulled herself together. Told herself she had to do this. Told herself it was nothing more than her job. She would be fine. Meeting new people was no problem at all, she tried to convince herself. Tucking the bag under her arm, taking a deep breath and clutching the edge of the shawl to try and still her shaking hands, Louise left the bedroom and walked down the stairs.

She needn't have worried so much about the dress. For Peter merely glanced up once as she walked towards him and said, 'Oh good, you're ready, let's be off then,' and he grabbed his car keys from the hall table and walked out of the front door. She followed out him into the night wondering how she had managed to become so invisible to her husband. The cold air chilled not only her body, but her heart.

They said little on the short drive to the Mess. She glanced at Peter, dressed in his best uniform, all buttons and braids, and the ice around her heart thawed a little. She thought how handsome he looked. How proud she was to be his wife. She very much hoped his awful episodes of dalliance with prostitutes were over. Maybe two of them dying had put him off, shaken him up, brought him to his senses. She certainly hoped so. Perhaps tonight would be the night they would experience the true meaning of being a married couple once again, for she'd never been able to resist him dressed in his finery and in the past neither had he, when she was dressed in hers.

The Officer's Mess looked wonderful and the sight of the gleaming glassware, cutlery and candles lifted Louise's spirits and a glass of wine warmed her a little. Waiters weaved in and out of the guests, trays of drinks held high, as everyone greeted their friends and colleagues.

She stood by Peter's side, smiling and nodding as he talked to everyone else and not to her. She felt his hand on her elbow a few times, as though he wanted to make sure she was still there. Towards the end of the melee that was drinks before dinner, she took a second glass of wine from a passing waitress.

'Are you sure you should have another one, dear?' Peter said without looking at her, his gaze travelling around the room. 'Maybe wait until dinner, eh?' and he glanced down, taking the glass out of her hand and placing it on a nearby table, before grabbing a whisky and downing it in one swallow. As he emptied his glass, the gong sounded for dinner. He gave the crystal tumbler to a waiter and held out his elbow.

'Shall we go in?' he said to the subordinates surrounding them, his smile encompassing them all. As they parted to allow the Colonel and his lady to pass first, Peter glanced down at her. The smile was still in place, but his eyes were hard. As if daring her to do anything but what was expected of her. So she took his proffered elbow and with a gracious nod of her head to his sycophants, allowed him to lead her into the dining room.

Louise assumed the food was good, it always was, but that night she tasted nothing. She simply chewed and swallowed. Chewed and swallowed. It was essential for her to maintain a steady rhythm; otherwise she was afraid she would lose her grip on her knife and fork and also on her sanity. She took his advice, though, and stayed clear of the alcohol, as she watched him down glass after glass. Whisky, wine (red and white), port and back to whisky again. She wondered if he would be able to stand when it was time to leave, for she couldn't have if she'd consumed that much alcohol.

At the end of the night, he was surprisingly pliable. They said their goodbyes and he managed to walk out of the Officers' Mess, clutching her arm. But this time not to keep her close, but to keep himself upright.

She drove the short distance back to their house in silence, her reflecting on the evening, he fast asleep, snoring. Once at the house, he walked up the stairs, went into the bedroom and promptly passed out on the bed, fully clothed. And there ended the evening.

Even though Louise had dressed up for him, looked beautiful, played the part of the Colonel's wife to perfection, it seemed it wasn't enough to tempt him. She clearly wasn't good enough. She was never good enough. It appeared that all that mattered to Peter was that she was there. By his side. Like some sort of mannequin. A parody of a member of the royal family, who did nothing more than smile, wave and occasionally incline a head. She didn't know what to do to get his attention. To get him to see her as a person, not the robot he obviously expected her to be.

She took off her beautiful dress, hanging it carefully in the wardrobe and pulled on a pair of pyjamas. She then cleaned her teeth and wiped away her makeup, before slipping between the icy sheets.

Thirty Seven

Walking into the Mess for a function, never failed to fill Crane with pride. Tonight was something different, though, a departure from the usual Mess nights. Some bright spark had come up with the idea of having a charity function. It was all about raising money for an Aldershot youth intervention charity which was doing good work in the local community. Trying to stop local youths from committing crimes and if they had, working with them towards giving their lives a new direction. Urging them to live a more positive way of life away from crime and gangs. A number of the boys had joined the army and were well on their way to becoming valued members of the forces.

Captain Draper loved the idea of the local garrison supporting this cause, especially as it was a particularly good fit for the military police and he therefore asked (army speak for told) that all his men and women of the rank of sergeant and above, attend the event. It also didn't hurt that a number of high ranking officers were also supporting the charitable evening and had thrown open the doors of the Officers' Mess for the occasion. Draper was also keen to raise the visibility and reputation of the military police in general and the SIB in particular.

Mingling with the other guests during the requisite drinks before the meal, Draper collared Crane and introduced Crane and Tina to Colonel Marshall, who had recently returned from Germany. The look that passed between Crane and Draper confirmed that this was no accidental meeting.

At the introduction, Crane said, 'Very pleased to meet you, sir. May I present my wife, Tina.'

Peter Marshall duly introduced his own wife, Louise and the two couples settled down to make small talk. Crane found this easy as he was particularly interested in the Colonel's time in Germany, as it wasn't without the realms of possibility that Crane would do a stint there one day. However, glancing over at his wife, Crane noticed Tina was struggling to make conversation with Louise Marshall.

'Do you have any children?' he heard Tina ask.

Louise Marshall mumbled her reply into her drink's glass, 'No, no, we don't.'

'Oh, what a shame,' said Tina. 'My little one, Daniel, is the light of my life. He's two now and growing like a weed. He's such a joy. We're not sure if we'll have any more yet, though...'

As Tina talked, her mouth running away with her, the Colonel's wife said less and less and Tina appeared to be trying her best to keep the conversation going. Mrs Marshall's face closed down. Her eyes went blank and she dropped her gaze away from Tina's face towards the drink in her hand.

It seemed the Colonel noticed his wife's problem as well, for he stopped talking to Crane mid-sentence and drew his wife away from them. As they moved away, the Colonel mumbled excuses about there being many others they had to meet that night.

Once on their own Tina hissed to Crane, 'That was like pulling teeth.'

'I saw you were having a bad time there.'

'Wasn't I just. I tried several topics until I hit on talking about children. But that seemed to make her worse. She shut down completely then.'

'There must be something going on there that we know nothing about,' Crane said and grabbed a glass off a passing tray.

'What was the Colonel like?' Tina asked him.

'Like every other Colonel, to be honest. He used a lot of words to say very little. They remind me of MPs, you know, officers.'

'Toeing the party line?'

'Exactly,' Crane grinned. 'They all say absolutely nothing of any importance. Oh and they never reply to a direct question.'

They both laughed and then the gong interrupted their conversation. It was time to take their seats for dinner.

Throughout the evening Crane watched Mrs Marshall, who was seated on a nearby table in his line of sight. She seemed uncomfortable all through the meal. She ate and drank very little. Spoke very little as well. She mostly sat with her hands in her lap, head slightly bowed, reminiscent of a quiet person of faith, as she let the whole evening wash over her head.

Occasionally she did raise her eyes to look at someone who was trying to draw her into conversation. He felt that he'd seen her, or her eyes before, but he just couldn't say when or where. She was definitely familiar, but Crane was unable to pin point why.

Thirty Eight

Ah, so you're back. I was hoping you would want to continue reading my story. So, stay with me awhile. I've more to tell. Let's continue our journey through the narrative of my life.

After I dealt with Doctor Harmon, all was quiet and stable for a while and my life took on a more conservative rhythm. I was emotionally drained from facing my past and bringing my tormentors to justice and took some time out to help me heal, both mentally and physically. I had thought my mission complete. I had had my retribution on the three men who had used and abused me. The men who had passed me from pillar to post and stolen my childhood.

I concentrated on the house. I buffed the wood to a new shine, cleaned the kitchen until it sparkled, banished the spiders and their cobwebs from both the cellar and the attic. I was happy. Well, as happy as I could be, I supposed. Perhaps resigned is a better description. I accepted my lot, such as it was. That was until I read an article in the local newspaper. See, here it is. I've cut it out and pasted it into the book, so you can read it for yourself

Joy for local couple

Fred and Sylvia Brown thought that they couldn't have children. After years of trying to get pregnant without success, Sylvia was finally diagnosed with blocked fallopian tubes, that it appeared could have been caused by a childhood illness. To help them come to terms with this terrible blow, the couple decided to selflessly devote their lives to others less fortunate than themselves. They had a large house and Fred Brown had a steady job that paid well, so they decided to share their good fortune. They became foster parents, raising young, needy and troubled children from differing backgrounds. The more disturbed the better, it seemed.

'We decided to take in those children who other foster parents wouldn't. The children we welcomed into our home had various issues. Anger. Despair. Loss. All of them were lonely, unloved, unwanted, confused and bewildered. Some stayed with us for several years, others only for a few weeks. We dedicated our lives to those children and it was a privilege to help them.'

And now after all the years of selfless sacrifice, Fred and Sylvia have become proud parents themselves.

'It's a miracle,' said Sylvia. 'Who would have thought it? A baby of our very own. We have looked after other people's children for years and years, taken in those whose own mothers had rejected them and now our reward is a child of our own. We are very fortunate and very thankful.'

Well, that's all very lovely, you might say. A bit cloying, a bit Disney all-American happy ending, but what has it to do with me? Well I'll tell you. I'll tell you the truth about Fred Brown. Show you the side of him that he hid from the world.

Louise turned the page of the red leather book expectantly. How alike they were, her and Matilda, Louise was realising more and more. Louise could relate to Matilda's description of her life. Feel her resignation. Understand her acceptance of her lot. Those were the words she'd use to describe herself; resigned and accepting. They were uncannily similar. There were parts of Louise's life that were good, her work in the community, the house, Matilda's book and others that...

The slam of the front door made her jerk her head up from Matilda's book. Peter? What on earth was he doing here? Louise scrambled off the bed, pushing the book underneath it. She was just straightening the pleats of the bed valance when he walked in to the bedroom.

'Hello,' she said, still on her knees by the side of the bed.

'Louise, what on earth are you doing?'

'Um, just, um. Well, I was dusting, you see and I knocked an ear ring off the bedside table and I'm trying to find it.' Louise hoped he wouldn't notice that there was no duster, or tin of polish. The two items she would need if she really were cleaning. 'Why are you here?' she asked, getting up from the floor.

'I left my mobile phone, it should be on the table there. If you've not knocked that off as well, that is.'

'No, no, here it is,' she picked up the mobile and handed it to him. 'See you later,' she said and got down on the floor again, continuing with her charade, running her hand over the carpet as though trying to find her lost piece of jewellery. The irony was not lost on her. For once she wanted rid of Peter, instead of the other way round.

Thirty Nine

The morning briefing over, Captain Draper relaxed, pushing back his chair and crossing his legs. Crane took the hint and relaxed back in his chair also.

'What did you think of the jamboree the other night then, Tom?'

'Thoroughly enjoyed it, boss, as did Tina.'

'Excellent. I thought it was a good idea of mine, to join in with a charity function. It also got the ranks together. Too often we are segregated and having been a Sgt Major before I took a commission, I have first-hand experience of the practice of keeping the ranks apart. So as a bit of an experiment, I think it worked rather well don't you think?'

'Yes, sir.' If Draper wanted his ego stroked, Crane was happy to oblige.

'It was interesting to meet the Colonel and Mrs Marshall, come to that. Had you met her before, Crane?'

'No, sir, I hadn't.'

'Striking woman, wouldn't you say, with that auburn hair, pale skin and green eyes,' Draper said.

And that's when the penny dropped. Crane sat stock

still in his chair, as though turned to stone. Trying to comprehend what had just popped unbidden into his mind. The image of the woman on the CCTV that Anderson had shown him. It was the eyes, those striking green eyes. The CCTV may be black and white but it couldn't hide the almond shape, or the long sweeping lashes.

Draper was still talking, but Crane didn't hear him. Draper stopped speaking and looked at Crane with the air of a perplexed man who had just seen his subordinate take absolutely no notice of him whatsoever.

'Crane, are you alright?'

'What? Oh, sorry, sir, yes, yes, I am. Or at least I think I am. I'm not altogether sure.'

'Stop spouting nonsense, Crane.'

Crane looked at his Captain. 'Sorry, sir, I need to speak to DI Anderson, urgently.'

And then Crane did something he'd never done in his life before. He walked out of the boss' office without being dismissed.

'Colonel Marshall's wife. Are you mad!' spluttered Anderson.

Crane had just completed a three mile journey in three minutes and was breathing hard from running into Aldershot Police Station and all the way up the office block to the CID offices. For some reason, in his madness, he'd thought the stairs would be quicker than the lift and had just run up five floors. Crane sat on a chair, ignoring the pile of papers already on it, which crinkled and crumpled beneath him.

'Yes, the Colonel's wife, Louise Marshall. There's something about her, Derek. I thought she was a bit strange when we met her at the function. Tina tried to talk to her, but she said very little. It was very definitely a one way conversation they had, with Tina doing all the talking. And he seems to speak for her, replies to questions for her. And another thing. He doesn't take much notice of her, but on the other hand, won't let her leave his side.'

'Okay, so they're a weird couple,' said Anderson. 'That doesn't mean anything, for as far as I can see most of you army types are weird.'

Crane ignored the dig and pulled two pieces of paper out of his black suit pocket. One was a page from the Aldershot News. He pointed to an article about the newly promoted Colonel and his wife.

'See here's their picture from the newspaper. What do you think? Can't you see the resemblance? The likeness between Mrs Marshall and the woman on the CCTV?'

Crane slapped down the second piece of paper, a still from the camera showing the woman near the KFC food outlet.

Anderson pointed to the news article. 'Crane, this woman is well bred, charming, refined. A prostitute? Or a killer of prostitutes? I think you've lost your mind to be frank.'

'Look beyond the clothes, look beyond the trappings of wealth,' Crane urged.

When he got no further comment from Anderson, Crane took a pair of scissors off Anderson's desk.

'What the hell are you doing?'

Crane cut the face out of both photos and placing them down on the top of the desk, put them next to each other, facing Derek.

'Well I'll be buggered,' said Anderson.

Forty

Anderson walked out of his office and barked orders at a couple of detective constables, reminding Crane suspiciously of himself and he wondered how much of the army was rubbing off on Derek, the more they worked together. Crane stood and wandered around the office, although turned in a circle was a more apt description, Anderson's work space hardly having room to swing a cat in. Piles of files littered the small space. They were on top of filing cabinets, chairs and strewn across the floor. He wondered where it all came from, as the police as well as the army were moving more towards paperless offices as the computer systems became ever more sophisticated. Perhaps they were the same files as he always saw there, a pile of filing waiting to be put away.

Derek returned with two mugs of tea and pulled an unopened packet of bourbon cream biscuits out of his desk drawer which they half emptied while they waited for the DC's to look over the CCTV footage they had of the red light area, to see what cars were driving towards the industrial estate in the previous 30 minutes to an hour before the approximate time of both deaths.

They were just about to start on the second half of the packet when a young man appeared at Anderson's door.

'Well?'

'You were right, Gov,' the young man said, the light of success shining in his eyes. 'A small dark hatchback was seen driving through the industrial area before each killing.'

'Any joy on the number plate?'

'No, sorry, can't see the plate clearly enough.'

'Oh well, worth a try,' said Anderson and stuffed another biscuit into his mouth.

'But there's something else you should know, sir. One of the other DC's that you asked to analyse the car number plates seen regularly in the area has just finished his report.'

'And?'

'And I think you'll be interested in this Lexus. It's a regular visitor to the area and it's registered to a Colonel Marshall, a resident of Aldershot Garrison.'

'You've got to be kidding me,' Anderson said as the young officer handed over a file and then retreated as Derek gesticulated for him to leave.

As Derek read over the report, a rather flustered Crane pulled out his mobile and had a quiet word with Staff Sgt Jones, asking him to ring him back with the information Crane needed. He was having trouble with the evidence he was being bombarded with in such a short space of time. Firstly the Colonel's wife's face and then the Colonel's car. It was all too much. He was beginning to think that he needed to lie down in a dark room.

While Anderson and Crane waited for Jones to call back, they mulled over what possible motives either of the Marshalls could have for killing prostitutes.

'She hates them?' said Anderson.

'Really? Is that the best you can come up with?'

'Husband hates them, then,' Anderson modified the thought.

'I suppose that would work,' said Crane. 'But why would he hate them? Why would the Colonel go around killing working girls? What possible reason could there be? And why would Louise Marshall be in the vicinity of the second killing? I grant you either of them could be driving the Lexus, but she's the only one who has been caught on camera.'

After a pause Crane said, 'Wait a minute, not he hates them, but he uses them…'

'And she kills them because of it,' Anderson finished the thought.

'A bit farfetched, though,' said Crane dismissing the possibilities that firstly the Colonel would use prostitutes and secondly that his wife would kill them because of it.

Crane's mobile rang interrupting their train of thought. For once it was a conveyor of good news. The Colonel couldn't be the one they were after, as he was away at the time of both murders, firstly on exercise and secondly at a conference. Crane felt the world settle back on its axis. His relief was palpable. But that still left him with the thorny question of Louise Marshall and her German-plated car that now had UK number plates.

Draper's initial reaction to Crane's theory was similar to Anderson's.

'You've got to be fucking joking!' Draper's choice of words rather more colourful than from Anderson.

'No, sir, I'm not,' said Crane. 'Here,' and he showed the two pictures to Draper who spent several moments studying them. He picked them up and held them to the light. He put them on his desk side by side. Crane thought at one point that Draper was going to get a magnifying glass out of his desk drawer and do a Sherlock Holmes impression.

But instead he said, 'Have you got any other evidence?'

'No, boss, I've not.'

'Well you better bloody get some if you insist on pursuing this.'

So it appeared Draper was prepared to take Crane seriously.

'How sir? Any thoughts?'

'Not my call, Crane. You want her, you get some evidence to catch her with. Rock solid, mind you. Oh, and don't let either her or the Colonel know what you're up to. Nor anyone else.'

'Can I get Billy to help me?'

'No. Find him something to do to keep him away from you. And tell no one else, only talk to DI Anderson or to me. Now fuck off.'

Forty One

The newspaper article had re-awoken the other me, the troubled me. The persona that lived deep inside of me. An alien. A beast that once woken had to be sated.

At least this would be a night time job, so I wouldn't be afraid of anyone seeing my face. According to the newspaper report, Fred and Sylvia Brown still lived in the same house, on the same street, in the same town. They must have been there for twenty years or more. I was fearful of returning to that house, I must confess. Afraid I would hear again the screams and cries of the children that had been placed with them by unsuspecting social workers. Once a child was in the clutches of Fred and Sylvia, it seemed to be a matter of out of sight, out of mind, by the authorities. The only way out was by running away and many of their victims were too traumatised to make a success of it. Whilst I was there a few tried, all failed. The Brown's house reminded me of a prisoner of war camp. We were all prisoners, resigned to our fate. It was as though we were awaiting the end of the war. Making the best of things until that far off, often dreamt of, day.

I arrived at the house about 3 am, late enough for everyone to have fallen asleep, yet early enough to ensure that no one would be waking up to start the day. I had managed to slip out of my house unseen, whilst my husband slept. I had no fear of him waking.

The sleeping tablet I had crushed and melted into his night-time whisky ensured it.

I knew the way into the Brown's house, of course. I'd been able to make my way in and out of the place without detection for years. It was an old house and the wooden windows didn't shut properly. All you needed was a bit of wire poked in through the gap and you could lift the latch. As I crept around to the back of the house, to the kitchen widow, I was relieved to find that the Brown's hadn't spent any of the money that they got from the state for looking after the foster children, on repairing the windows. And so my old trick from years ago worked. I opened the window and climbed in.

I turned on the small torch I had brought with me, using it to light my way, but keeping the beam on the floor. I knew every creak and groan in that house and so was able to make my way up the wooden stairs with the minimum of noise. My feet slipping into their old pattern as easily as if there were footsteps painted on the carpet for me to follow.

I made my way to the nursery. I had to be extra careful. The baby's room was next door to Fred and Sylvia's. The door was open, thank goodness, as I knew that was the one whose hinges creaked. Slipping in through the opening, I took tentative steps across the room until I was at the cot.

I looked down on him. He was a beautiful child, that innocent boy, sleeping the sleep of the righteous. But I wondered how long it would take for him to become as foul and vile as his parents. He was lying on his back, head turned to one side. I reached out and ran my hand over his hair. It was the finest, softest thing I had ever touched. With the smallest of sobs stuck in my throat, I impaled him through the heart with a shard of glass.

Forty Two

The shock of what she'd just read, made Louise drop the book. It clattered to the floor, and she left it where it fell. A pool of red on the floor, the colour of the baby's blood that had been spilled. Louise stood and backed away from it, her mind a maelstrom of thoughts. Emotions swirled through her; hatred, anger, sorrow.

How could Matilda have done that? Taken the life of a child? Louise could understand the other murders. They were acts of revenge, necessary retribution. Call it what you would they were, in their way, understandable. Do unto others as they do unto you, flitted through her mind. A piece of scripture she had heard in bible readings at one garrison church or another. Matilda had obviously taken this as her mantra. But this time Louise felt that Matilda had gone too far.

Louise grabbed the white headscarf and wrapped the book up in it. She needed to get it out of her sight. If nothing else, she needed to cover up the blood red of the cover. She placed it on the chair, determined to return it to its hiding place. Her hands were shaking. Louise longed for a cigarette. Smoking was a filthy habit she had given up years ago. Yet they said the craving never went away completely. The way she was feeling at that moment confirmed that. But she didn't even have a lighter in the house never mind a cigarette. She felt like an alcoholic desperate for a drink. Just one to make the jitters go away. If she'd had a packet of cigarettes in the house, that's what she would have done, had just one.

In the absence of nicotine, she fancied the next best thing would be coffee. Caffeine would be a good alternative and she hurried into the kitchen to put the coffee pot on, leaving the book on the chair. The making of the coffee soothed her. Her well-practiced movements, the normalcy of the everyday task, brought her back from her horror and revulsion. As the smell of coffee permeated the kitchen, she thought that perhaps she would go back to the book. Once she had a crutch with her. For surely Matilda would have had a good reason for doing what she did. The woman who wrote the book, whom Louise had become so close to and regarded as a friend, didn't kill without good reason.

As she poured the freshly brewed, fragrant coffee, her hands were steady, her breathing had returned to normal, in anticipation of reading Matilda's explanation.

Forty Three

Why did I do that? You must be asking yourself that question. How I could kill an innocent baby? You must be outraged. But there is a reasonable, rational, explanation. I may be the emotionally ravaged, desperate woman they have turned me into. The sum of all their abuses. But the Brown's inflicted perhaps the worst abuse of all. Or rather Fred Brown did. I killed their baby, because he had killed mine.

I became pregnant with my foster father's baby. That charming, smiling man, a pillar of the local community would come to my room at night and force himself on me. I once tried to tell Mrs Brown. But as I endeavoured to get the awful words out, force them from a mouth that was tongue-tied, she shot me a look of pure hatred. It was then that I realised she knew. She was complicit in his unspeakable, disgusting behaviour. She grabbed my arm and pulled me close to her. Through a mouth that had turned from a smile into a snarl, she hissed in my ear. Told me not to tell anyone. For no one would believe me, she said. Her and her husband would make sure everyone knew what a filthy liar I was. They would say that I wasn't to be trusted. Explain that I had these awful fantastical thoughts that were made up. They would call me a poor child who was so tormented by past treatment that I didn't know fantasy from reality. But it would be alright. They would keep me on, despite my terrible lies, for they wouldn't give up on me.

Although I hated Fred Brown, I loved the thought of having a child. The one thing that I could call my own. Someone who I could be close to and love, for I had never known love in my pitiful life before. So I heaped all the love in my soul on the baby growing inside me. I didn't tell anyone. It was my secret. I hugged it to me for several months, until I began to show, that was. When no longer the baggy oversized clothes I hid in, could conceal my growing stomach. One night when Fred took to my bed, he realised I was pregnant. He felt my breasts that were growing and swelling with milk. Ran his hands over the mound of my stomach. He got out of bed and stood over me. I pleaded with him not to hurt me, not to hurt my unborn child. But he took no notice. He slapped me across the face and told me to keep my filthy mouth shut. Grabbed me by the arm and dragged me off the bed so I landed on the floor with a thump. Then he kicked me repeatedly in the stomach, until his anger was sated and he left me bruised and bleeding on my bedroom floor.

The next day I lost my baby. My son. Aborted from my body by the thug who had impregnated me. As the baby was ripped out of my body, so was the love I had never felt before. Both fledging things, ready for ripening. Now shrivelled and lifeless. I was never the same after that.

Maybe now you can understand why I killed his baby, for he had killed mine. It was their turn to feel the pain, to be tormented by the loss. Their turn to have the one thing they loved more than anything else, ripped from them.

Forty Four

Louise closed the book. She was overwhelmed with emotion that she couldn't contain. She curled up into a ball and allowed herself to feel everything that had been suppressed for so long. Emotions that had remained dormant for years bubbled up, refusing to be buried any longer.

And so Louise cried over Matilda's story. She couldn't believe that anyone could go through what Matilda had and remain sane. Her friend (for that's what she considered Matilda to be) had been through more pain in her life than surely anyone could bear. It was as though all the evil in the world had descended upon her.

Louise sobbed for the two dead babies. Sobbed for babies everywhere. Sobbed for the babies she would never have. Sobbed for the maternal love she would never know. By now she was losing control of her emotions, she was becoming hysterical.

Forcing herself to calm down, taking huge gulping breaths interspersed with sobs, she uncurled from the chair and staggered into the kitchen, as though drunk. She was intoxicated, although not with alcohol but with emotion. She ran the tap and filled a glass with water. But before drinking it, she splashed the cold water on her face. Held her wet hands against her eyes, which were swollen and burning.

Not bothering to dry her face, Louise sipped the water and considered how alike they were, the two women who had never met, but whose stories were so similar. She felt an affinity with her, felt that Matilda was a kindred spirit. Louise only knew Matilda's name. Didn't know if she was still alive. Didn't yet know what had happened to her. But Louise was convinced they were as one.

Forty Five

Peter was also intoxicated, excited beyond reason. He'd practically run out of the house that evening, away from Louise, out into the welcoming dark. As he started the car and drove away, leaving Louise behind at home, his thoughts were focused on his destination. The red light district called him once more. He'd tried to stop seeing the prostitutes, he really had, especially after his first two girls were killed. But he was addicted, he knew that now. He embraced the knowledge. He embraced his addiction. He supposed he was like a drug addict, a gambler, an alcoholic. It didn't matter what your addiction was, the substance was all that mattered. The drugs, the money, the alcohol, or in his case, the sex. Reason went out of the window. He'd found the fear of being caught just heightened the experience. Waiting in a queue of traffic at a red light, his heel tapped rapidly on the floor of the car and he wrung the steering wheel with his hands over and over again.

At home, or at work, when he was rational, normal, he could see how his predilection could harm him. Harm his career and his marriage. For both went hand in hand. As the lights changed to green and he was on the move once more, he reflected that he was good at his job, but so was Louise. She was as good at hers as he was at his. The higher one climbed up the officer ranks, the more important a good wife became. Some would call it old fashioned, he guessed. Out dated. Over rated. But in his world, Louise was an integral part of his success.

It's just that he didn't see her as a woman anymore, he supposed. She was more like one of his officers. She had her role to play and he expected her to play it to his exacting, high standards. She was just part of the machinery that was the army. That was his life.

Which only served to highlight the difference between Louise and the prostitutes. Since Sally and Lindsay had died, he'd been seeing another girl called April. She had helped him with his grief. Helped him see that there was light at the end of the tunnel. See that the girls' deaths weren't the end, but just one point on his journey through life.

He supposed April looked a little like Louise. Slim build, brunette, heart shaped lips. But whereas Louise was prim and proper, the prostitute was full of life. Louise was weak, whining and older. Her desperation made him feel sick. She hung onto him, her eyes imploring him to want her. But it was her need that turned him off. By contrast April was eager, sexy, forward and young. He couldn't resist her. He knew he wouldn't stop seeing her. He couldn't stop. He just couldn't help it and his foot pressed harder on the accelerator in anticipation of their meeting.

Forty Six

Louise was watching. She was sitting in her car, a little way down the road and on the opposite side, as her husband drew his car to a stop by the line of girls plying their wares, who were all displaying what they thought were their best attributes. They stood, posed. Some of them had one leg in front of the other, chin slightly down, cheeks sucked in. Others had hands on their hips, pushing their breasts forward. Breasts that were barely covered by the lace and silk clothing they wore. Others were leaning forwards, bent at the waist, displaying tiny thongs that didn't leave much to the imagination. But Peter didn't seem interested in them. His head swivelled as he scanned the line-up and it didn't take long before a girl ran up to the car and climbed in.

Louise's anger and hatred was building. Anger at the girls who flaunted their sexuality and sold themselves for money. Hatred against the prostitutes who were stealing her husband away from her. It was clear to Louise that Peter's eyes were oblivious to his wife now. His sight blinkered, eyes clouded as though he had cataracts. He must no longer see Louise as a woman.

No longer see her as a sexual partner.

Normally she went home once Peter had made his choice, but this time she stayed. Waited. She was unable to dampen down the fuse that her anger had lit. Unable to stop the process that Peter had unwittingly begun. Glad that she was ready. Glad that she'd adhered to Peter's principal of being ready for anything. To always be prepared. A past memory of being in the Girl Guides flittered through her mind. Be prepared. That motto had echoed throughout her life.

It had been the eyes that had done it, Louise thought. The whore's eyes had lit up when she'd seen Peter's car. She'd run towards it, climbed into the passenger seat and turned to him. And then he'd kissed the girl. Right there in front of everyone. The other girls had smirked. Cat-called to him, called him a dirty old man, teased the young girl about the dangers of getting too fond of a regular.

And because of that Louise had stayed, maintained her lonely vigil. Waited until he'd come back and returned his favourite prostitute to the line-up. So she could continue her disgusting work. So she could continue tempting more husbands away from their wives.

Louise watched as the young whore got out of the car, putting the money Peter had just given her into her purse and called to the others girls that she was just going to get a coffee. As she disappeared around the corner and Peter drove away, Louise got out of her car. She followed the girl down the side street and saw her go into a brightly lit cafe. Louise stood a little way back, in the shadows, as the whore approached the serving counter and spoke to the woman behind it.

Instant coffee was spooned into a large take away

cup and milk was steam heated and then poured on top. There were no other customers in the establishment, which looked as though it was a throwback to the 1960's. It looked like a typical working man's cafe; Formica topped tables, plastic chairs fastened to the floor, menus adorning the walls. Starbucks it was not.

As the girl came out with the take away cup, the street was empty. She walked up the side street to join her... what would you call them, Louise mused? Co-workers? Colleagues? She smirked to herself. Whatever they were called, they'd be missing one of their number any minute now.

Louise pushed herself off the wall, walked up to the prostitute and knocked against her, spilling the drink and scalding the girl's hands and arms.

She looked up at Louise. 'What the fuck did you do that for?' she asked. 'Look at me, I'm covered in the bloody stuff and it hurts like hell.'

'Because I needed to get your attention,' said Louise.
'Why?'
'So I could do this,' Louise replied and stabbed the whore through the heart with her shard of glass.

Forty Seven

'999 what's your emergency?'

The operator was treated to a volley of screams. They sounded female, so he said, well shouted, actually, 'What's happened, love? You've got to tell me, so I can help you.'

He was rewarded with the sounds of sobs, then gulps, then the voice said, 'It's my friend April. I think she's dead.'

'What makes you think that?'

'Because she's got a bloody great piece of glass sticking out of her chest! Is that a good enough reason?'

'Yes, that's a good enough reason.' The operator knew that the best way of dissolving the caller's anger was to repeat back to the girl what she'd said, as if agreeing with her. 'I'll send out an ambulance. Now tell me where you are.'

The girl managed to give him a street name in Aldershot. 'I'm just down from the all night cafe,' she finished.

The operator had been typing on his console all the time she was talking and so could reply with, 'The ambulance is on its way. Can you stay there please and direct the paramedics?'

'Um, not sure I can, it's, it's,' he could hear sobs starting again. 'It's so horrible, you know?'

Luckily the operator didn't know, but again had to agree. 'Yes, I know it must be very upsetting for you. Can you move just a short distance away from April until they get there?'

'Uh, oh, okay,' and he could hear her footsteps that sounded like horse hooves over the echoing mobile phone line.

'Stay on the phone with me until they get there. They're only a couple of minutes out now, okay?'

'Yes, I suppose so.'

While the man was talking to the girl, he was also dispatching a police car to the scene, without telling her. He knew the area she was calling from was the Aldershot red light area. She was more than likely a prostitute, as was her dead friend. He didn't want the girl to do a runner, which she might do if she knew he'd called the police. He was sure the local coppers would want to interview her.

Then through the line he could hear sirens, firstly in the distance and gradually getting louder. 'Sounds like they're close, can you see the ambulance yet?'

'Yes, it's seen me. It's here. They're getting out now.'

'Okay, thank you so much, the ambulance personnel will take over now. Goodbye and good luck.'

He was about to add that he hoped her friend was okay, but knew that was far from likely and he cleared the call, then pressed a new button on his console and said, '999. What's your emergency?'

Forty Eight

As the police traffic car pulled to a halt behind the ambulance, skidding slightly on the wet road from the incessant drizzle that had set in about 30 minutes before, PC Colin Daniels grabbed his door, opened it and ran to the incident, leaving his less experienced colleague to turn off the engine and report to control that they had arrived. As he drew near, he could see a cluster of paramedics and civilians around someone lying on the damp ground. A girl by the looks of her long legs and high heeled shoes, that he could just glimpse through the crowd. As he heard his fellow police officer arrive at his shoulder, puffing and panting, the people around the girl parted, like the red sea, giving PC Daniels and his partner a full on view of the horrific scene before them.

A week ago the nightly briefing had included details of local prostitutes being murdered with a shard of glass, urging them to be vigilant when patrolling around the industrial area of Aldershot. Even Daniels, although not a detective, could see this incident had the same MO as the others. He stepped forward and had a quiet word with a paramedic. Then speaking into his shoulder mike he said, '746 to control, we have a code 187. Requesting back-up and patch me through to DI Anderson.'

After a few garbled replies and the odd hiss and click, Anderson's voice came through the mike. 'Attending an incident in the red light district, sir,' Daniels said, having to raise his voice over the sound of his young partner throwing up in the gutter. 'Looks like this is another one for you, sir. We've got a girl with a piece of glass sticking out of her.'

'Fuck,' was Anderson's reply.

'Couldn't agree more, sir. Anyway, an ambulance is on the scene, but they can't do anything for her.'

'Are you sure?' Anderson said.

'Very, sir. They can't do CPR as the glass appears to have pierced her heart and they can't feel a pulse. We're waiting for the doc to arrive to call her dead at the scene. I've called for back-up and I'm about to cordon the area off.'

'Well get on with it and stop talking to me before anyone else corrupts my crime scene. And get the bloody ambulance crew out of the way!'

'Will do, sir,' and Daniels cut the connection and went to do Anderson's bidding, thinking that the detective could have asked nicely. But also knowing that was all the thanks a foot soldier would get from a detective.

By the time Crane arrived, Major Martin was already there and the crime scene tent had been erected. Crane wrapped his coat around him to ward off the chill of the night and the drizzle and waited for Anderson to come out of the tent.

He wandered around as he waited, puffing on a

cigarette and looking at the crowd that had gathered. Gawkers, upset girls, thwarted customers, were all craning their necks to try and get a glimpse of something. Anything. Perhaps they were waiting for the news vans to arrive so they could be interviewed as 'concerned locals'.

When Anderson emerged from the tent, he shuffled and crinkled his way over to Crane in his white suit.

'Another one then?' Crane said.

'Afraid so,' said Anderson. 'Want a look?'

'Nah, not this time. I'll look at the photos tomorrow. Any CCTV cameras around?' Crane looked up at the nearby buildings expectantly.

'A few. I've already called for footage from any cameras in the vicinity to be pulled as soon as possible by the CCTV centre in Farnborough.'

'So if we find there's nothing conclusive on the CCTV again,' Crane said, 'Please tell me you've got some forensics this time?' Being rather fed up of finding young girls dead in the street with glass used to cut them open, his tone reflected his frustration.

'Nothing here, so far, yet again, I'm afraid.' Anderson looked as pissed off as Crane. 'But late this afternoon I had a report from the laboratory on the clothes from the first girl who was killed. We've a couple of finger prints. They were on a shoe and don't belong to Sally Smith, or any of her friends, we've checked. It was easily done as they're all on file having been arrested at one point or another for soliciting.'

'Brilliant, we've got prints, but at the moment you can't find a match?'

'No.'

After thinking for a moment, Crane came to a decision. 'In that case,' he said, 'I'm going to have to help you out, aren't I?'

'How are you going to do that?'

'Best you don't know, Derek. I'll be in touch.'

'Don't you want to interview the girl who found the body with me?'

'No need,' Crane said, 'I'm sure you're more than capable,' and he wandered back to his car, still deep in thought.

Forty Nine

Louise ran away from the girl she'd just killed, before she realised that she should walk. Quickly, but walk. She didn't want to draw unnecessary attention to herself. She managed to get to her car unseen. At least she hoped she had. But as she opened the car door and sat in the driver's seat, the courtesy light revealed that she was covered in blood. Dark, sticky patches covered her camel wool coat and there was blood on her gloves and up her wrists. This was the first time it had happened and Louise was beginning to panic. Sticking glass into the eye of Sally and the ear of Louise hadn't been nearly as messy. This last girl had been a bit of a crime of opportunity and she hadn't given any thought to her clothes. At the time, she had just been glad that she had taken the precaution of putting her gloves on and that she had her glass shard under the car seat.

The coppery smell of the bloody made her gag and she ripped off the gloves and went to throw them out of the window, before realising she couldn't do that as they had to be hidden or destroyed and so she had no choice but to drop them in her lap. She couldn't take her coat off either yet until she found somewhere safe to dispose of it. She wondered if there was any blood on the car upholstery, or on the car door, but deciding that there was nothing she could do about it for now, she started the car.

Jerking away from the curb, it took a few moments to get her emotions under control, while the car kangarooed drunkenly along the road. But by the time she arrived at the edge of the industrial area, she had calmed down sufficiently to drive properly. Instead of turning left and going home, she turned right to divert around Farnborough, heading for the edge of the shopping centre. There she parked the car and managed to dump her gloves and coat underneath some restaurant rubbish in a large industrial sized bin. She hurried back to the car, not noticing that as she'd stuffed the clothes into the bin, a leather glove had dropped onto the road.

Peter arrived back at the house, wearing a grin of satisfaction, as wide as April's legs, all the way home. When he pulled into the drive, cutting the engine and coasting his way to the door, he was surprised to find that Louise's car wasn't in its usual place on the drive. But instead of being concerned he just shrugged and was glad, for that meant there would be no row about him having been out all evening.

As he walked into the house, the lights were still on, although the television had been turned off. He walked into the kitchen which was spotless as usual. He wondered where Louise had gone to and thought perhaps she had nipped out for coffee or a drink with a friend. But he dismissed that idea. Louise didn't have friends, just the wives of his officers and she certainly wouldn't think of going to any one of those for support, if she was pissed at him that was. That sort of behaviour would never do. A more realistic thought was that she must have gone for a drive, to ward off the boredom or the sadness. If that was the case, at least the tears would be shed elsewhere and not at home.

But then he had an epiphany. For he realised that he didn't much care where she was and that thought made him wonder when he'd stopped loving his wife. Since coming to the Garrison, he realised. It was the house, or Aldershot, or the new job, or the girls. Take your pick. It could be any of those. Obviously he would be concerned if she was hurt or injured in a car accident or anything, but he was sure she was fine.

Peeling off his clothes in the upstairs bathroom, Peter had a quick shower. As Louise was still not home when he finished, he went to bed feeling pleasantly weary after his night time exertions and fell asleep without giving his wife another thought. He drifted off to sleep with the feel of April still on his lips and the smell of her perfume in his nostrils.

Fifty

First thing the next morning, upon arriving at Provost Barracks, Crane stood for a while mulling over the incident boards that he'd insisted on setting up, even though the murder investigations were primarily a police matter. Crane had his method of working, which had served him well in the past and he didn't intend to change it. He had a mug of freshly brewed black coffee in his hand and as he savoured the taste and the aroma, he studied each board in turn and ticked off in his mind the salient points.

The first death had been that of prostitute Sally Smith. She was stabbed through the eye with a shard of glass. No forensic evidence was found at the scene. A small dark hatchback was seen on CCTV and witnesses said the number plate was German. They had two finger prints that were found on Sally's shoe, as yet unable to find a match for them. No family members had been identified.

The second murder had been that of Lindsay Hatton, Sally's friend and fellow working girl. She had been stabbed through the ear by the side of the KFC in the town centre. Again a dark hatchback type car was seen in the vicinity. Again they had no forensic evidence, not even a finger print this time. Again they were unable to trace Lindsay's parents.

The latest murder victim was April Shower. Crane wondered if her parent's had given her that name, or if she had adopted it. She was very young. Last night Major Martin reckoned she was only about 16, so maybe it was her non-de-plume, a name she thought was cool. This murder was much messier, April having been stabbed through the heart, again with a shard of glass. It was a much dirtier, disordered scene than the previous two as well and Crane knew they had to find the killer's clothes. There would have been a lot of blood on them. Major Martin would no doubt find bits from a dark coloured leather glove on the glass, during the post mortem this morning. Crane put a question mark against the gloves. They must be somewhere. But where? It was too early yet for the CCTV footage to have been isolated and viewed so he could only put a question mark against that as well.

With nothing else to add for the time being, Crane went upstairs to brief his boss, Captain Draper on the latest murder.

Once he'd done that, Crane then voiced his suspicions to Draper that Mrs Marshall must be involved somewhere along the line. The car was right, even if the number plate was wrong and she'd been in Aldershot at the time of the first and second murders. Tellingly, the Colonel was away at the same time.

'Mind you, the Colonel was here in Aldershot last night,' Crane finished.

'Oh, so you've checked already?' asked Draper, who seemed to be trying to stop a grin spreading and only succeeded in looking as though he were taking part in a gurning competition, his face twisting this way and that as he strained to keep control.

'Of course, sir, I wouldn't be doing my job properly if I hadn't,' Crane grinned back. 'I suppose I could calculate the time taken for the Colonel to leave where ever he was at the time of the first two murders, come back to Aldershot, murder the girls and then go back again.'

'Don't waste your time, Crane. He was with his officers most of the time on both occasions.'

'Alright, boss, well in that case it just leaves Mrs Marshall.'

'Well, in order to try and build a case against her, you're going to have to get some forensic evidence, or at least a match to those finger prints. But I'm warning you now, Crane, you're not to go anywhere near the Colonel or his wife without something solid. Do you understand? No interviews, no taking them to the police station, no questioning.'

'Yes, sir, I promise not to accuse either them of anything, not even a driving offence, without clear forensic evidence.'

'Very well, dismissed.'

Fifty One

It was mid-morning. Not having any wifely duties that day, Louise had finished her chores and then decided to reward herself with reading another instalment in the story of Matilda's life. She was just fishing the book out from the back of her wardrobe when the doorbell rang. She hastily returned the book to its hiding place and went to answer the door.

The man looked vaguely familiar. He wasn't dressed in uniform, but rather in a dark suit, white shirt and dark tie. Ah, the Branch, she said to herself.

'Yes? Can I help you?' she spoke out loud.

'Sorry to bother you, ma'am, I don't know if you remember me? Sgt Major Crane? We met at the recent charity function.'

'Oh so we did. Hello, Sgt Major. What can I do for you?'

Louise was all smiles, graciousness personified, although her heart was beating so hard in her chest, she was afraid he could see it bumping against her sweater. The sound of it filled her head until she thought it would burst.

'Sorry, ma'am but my car has overheated.'

'I can't see any car.' Louise's pulse rate went from a trot to a canter.

'It's in the road behind your house. I wonder could you fill my water container.'

'I, um...' Louise could see the strange way he was looking at her, just that little too closely. He seemed to be honing in on her face as if trying to gauge her reaction. What was he seeing? Her pulse rate increased yet again, from a canter to a gallop.

Crane held out the container, holding the bottom, so she could take the handle.

'Yes, of course, one moment,' Louise said and took the container.

She left the door open and walked to the kitchen, knowing that he wouldn't come in. Wouldn't follow her indoors. He wouldn't dare enter an officer's house, especially not the Colonel's. Not without an invitation and one wasn't about to be offered.

In the kitchen, she filled the water container from the tap, and then wiped her prints off it using a tea towel. She returned to the front door, holding the container handle with the towel underneath her fingers.

'Here it is, Sgt Major. Sorry, I made a bit of a mess. I managed to spill water everywhere and had to wipe it up. I hope your car is alright,' she finished, putting the plastic container on the ground. As he bent to pick it up she closed the door on him, leaning against it as she listened to him crunch his way back down the gravel drive.

Her thoughts raced in time with her pulse. What the hell was that all about? She was convinced Crane had been trying to get her fingerprints, but why? What possible reason would he have for suspecting her? She'd changed the number plate on her car, from the

English back to the German one each time she'd gone out looking for the whores. She couldn't remember ever taking her gloves off. She walked to the kitchen on unsteady legs racking her brain for any failure on her part. And then it hit her. Like a punch in the face. Dazed, she realised that during the first murder she'd only had time to slip on one glove onto the hand that she'd held the shard of glass in, for it would have looked peculiar if she'd kept her gloves on after leaving the car. It might have made the prostitute suspicious.

In her mind she replayed her movements. She'd grabbed the blanket from the back seat of the car, picking up her gloves and shard of glass that she'd hidden underneath it, taking care only to hold the glass with the rug and not her bare hands. She'd laid the rug out on the grass, hiding the gloves and glass beneath it. Before turning to lean over the girl, she'd slipped on a glove and grabbed the glass. Then, when it was over, she'd rolled the girl off the rug and automatically picked up the shoe that had fallen off and replaced it on the girl's foot. Louise realised she had used the wrong hand to do that with. She'd used the hand that hadn't had the glove on.

Louise wasn't sure how much time she had left. How long it would take them to gather enough evidence to charge her. She knew there was a major investigation underway. She'd seen the papers and the local television news. She'd seen her husband stiffen as he read each article in the Aldershot News and then look up at her. Was there an unspoken question in his eyes? Did he suspect her? Was he beginning to think she knew about his disgusting filthy habit of using prostitutes? Had he seen her car following him in his rear view mirror?

She'd seen through Crane's ruse, of course. Did he think her stupid? What a bloody pathetic attempt at getting her fingerprints that had been. Maybe they'd traced the German plate? Traced it back to her somehow? Why else would Crane have come?

But she couldn't let them take her. Not just yet. She needed a little while longer. She needed to finish the book. She ran upstairs and took the volume from the back of the wardrobe. She didn't bother to go downstairs to read it, or to make a coffee first. She couldn't risk the time it would take. She jumped up on the bed and opened it. She was calming down now, her breathing returning to normal. Her anxiety faded into the background as she focused on Matilda's words. The book would tell her what to do next. Matilda would show her the way.

Fifty Two

It's nearly time to claim my last victim. The one who could have been the first, but the one I decided to leave until last. I wanted to anticipate the moment, I suppose. Turn it over in my mind. Plan the perfect execution. Savour the build-up. Knowing that I was going to kill him, and he didn't. He had no idea what was coming. No idea how I felt behind the everyday wifely mask I wore for him. What would he see behind that mask should it ever be ripped off? Would my husband see my hurt and pity me? Would he see evil and be afraid of me? Would he understand the part he had played in making what he would no doubt perceive as a monster?

And so I waited. Honed my killing skills until I was ready for him. Practiced on the others you might say. Made sure I knew what I was doing and would be able to execute my plan to perfection.

You might wonder what his crime against me was. Why I should want to snuff out my husband's beating heart. It is because he is the one who has enslaved me for the rest of my life. The others, the priest, the headmaster, the doctor and Fred Brown, they all abused me as a child. He now abuses me as a woman.

How did I end up here, in this house, with him you might ask. Well it went like this. My childhood years eventually ran out. I became too old for my tormentors, for they were paedophiles who only liked young flesh. Once I grew up, they didn't find me attractive anymore. But instead of throwing me out with the rubbish, leaving me to my own devices, letting me take my chances in the wide world, they sold me. Sold my body and soul for a few lousy quid. And so I came to this house, to this man, to this garrison, to the army. With nothing more than my battered chest that contained a few paltry possessions.

But it was the house, in the end, that was my salvation. It offered me protection, succour and shelter. I felt that I had come home. And so under the calming influence of its tiled roof, encased within its rich warm red brick walls, I can finally be myself. I can never leave here. I will stay forever.

Fifty Three

PC Colin Daniels was driving the patrol car, unable to take much more of his young colleague's driving that night. He was fed up of Ben being in the wrong gear, taking corners too fast or too slowly and getting stuck behind dawdling drivers. So he'd decided to take control for the last few hours of their shift. He did it nicely, of course, without criticism. He merely offered to give the young man a break.

It was fast approaching the end of their shift at 10pm and Daniels was looking forward to getting back to the station and the waiting hot cup of tea as he rounded a corner near the Farnborough shopping centre. He'd followed the road around the outskirts of the centre, checking for kids hanging around in groups, perhaps hassling unsuspecting dog walkers or spraying their stupid graffiti. He didn't mind graffiti per say, it's just that it had to be good. And the kids around Farnborough were not Banksy. Stupid tag names and strange symbols were all they seemed to be able to manage and the Town Council were fed up of cleaning the stuff off during the day, only to see it pop up again the next night. So they had asked the local police to try and nip it in the bud if they found any kids with spray paint cans.

As Daniels swung around to the entrance of the centre on his right hand side and the car park on his left, he saw some spray painting on the corner of the first shop in the precinct. Sighing and pulling over he said to Ben, 'I'll just check out that tag there, won't be a minute,' and he clambered out as quickly as he could, encumbered as he was by his uniform and stab vest.

Walking through the wind that was coming down the street, he approached the offending spray paint to try and identify the kids who'd done it. As he walked up to it, he had to veer around a large industrial rubbish bin. And that's when something caught his eye. A flash of brown on the floor between the wall and the bin. Bending down he saw it was a discarded glove and he was just about to pick it up, when he noticed dark stains on it. Stepping backwards he turned and waved his colleague over. Leaving the young boy standing there guarding the find, he went back to the patrol car and called it in, requesting a forensic team to come and collect the glove that had what looked like blood stains on it, from the floor behind the rubbish bin.

DI Anderson wasn't far behind them and walked over to PC Daniels on his arrival.

'Colin,' he nodded. 'Good find.'

'Thank you, sir.' Daniels was genuinely pleased with Anderson's acknowledgement. Perhaps the detectives weren't such arses after all.

'So, what's the status?'

'Well, sir, forensics are photographing the glove in-situ and have confirmed that on initial examination it is blood stained. They've checked the bin itself but unfortunately the rubbish collection has already taken place, so if there was anything else of interest in there, any other items or clothes, they've already gone to the landfill.'

'So all we have is the glove.'

'Afraid so, sir. As the ground is tarmac, there's no chance of footprints, but they're dusting the bin itself for finger prints.'

'That could take all night,' Anderson laughed. 'God knows how many they'll find. Not sure I'd like that job.'

'Exactly, sir.

'Anyway, you can get off now,' Anderson said. 'Control wants you back at the police station to hand over to the next crew,' and with another nod Anderson headed over to the bin.

As Colin walked back to the car, his young partner was bubbling over with excitement.

'Bloody hell, Colin, we could have cracked the case here. Who'd have thought we'd be instrumental in finding the killer?' Ben said.

Colin though the 'we' was a bit of a stretch, but kept quiet.

'Just wait till I get home,' Ben continued. 'I can't wait to tell Julie all about it. She'll be dead excited too.'

Colin stopped walking. 'Who's Julie?' he asked.

'My sister. She always wants to know what I've been up to at work.'

'Right,' Colin said. 'Let's get one thing straight. Right now. This minute.'

Ben had also stopped walking and was looking up at his older, far more experienced partner.

'You tell no one. Do you hear?' Colin's words came out rather harsher than he'd intended, but, on the other hand, he reasoned, Ben had to realise the importance of his message.

Ben nodded enthusiastically, the tips of his ears burning red. 'Yes, sorry.'

'Walls have ears,' Colin said. 'As do the press. Once you tell one person, they'll tell another five, who'll tell another ten. Get the idea?'

Ben nodded bashfully.

'Before you know it, the information has fallen into the wrong hands. It'll be all over the papers and the internet. And that could alert the killer. So tell no one. Right?'

'Right, Colin. Sorry.' Ben paused for a moment, and then said, 'But it's still bloody exciting!'

Daniels followed Ben to the car, shaking his head and wondering when he'd lost the excited feeling Ben was currently displaying for the job.

Fifty Four

Crane and Anderson were sat in Anderson's office at Aldershot Police Station the next morning with cups of tea in front of them. Anderson was munching on a biscuit. He'd offered one to Crane, but it was too early in the morning for him.

'Right,' Anderson said. 'The glove found last night has been sent to the laboratory for forensic examination. So far all we have is that the blood on it is the same type as the latest victim April. Obviously they are running DNA tests on it, just to be sure it's hers, but that test will take a while yet.'

'Can they check for any skin cells or anything inside the glove they can get a trace on?' Crane asked.

'We're ahead of you there. It turns out there's a small spot of blood inside the glove, they are trying to get DNA from it.'

'So it could be the killer's blood?'

'Maybe,' Anderson nodded, 'Perhaps from a small cut from the glass. It's worth a try at any rate.'

'But if it is the killer's and it's from the same person as the fingerprints on Sally's shoe, then we won't get a match. We've not got those prints on file, so it stands to reason we won't have the DNA either.'

'I know, but we'll have it for future reference. To confirm the killer, once we have a suspect.'

'And there's the rub,' said Crane.

His ruse to get Mrs Marshall's fingerprints had failed. If he was honest, it had made him feel really stupid. He hoped he hadn't done anything to hinder the investigation, but thinking about it, why would he have done? But not really knowing, he decided to push the uncertain thoughts away and focus on what they could do something about.

'What CCTV have you got?' Crane asked Anderson. 'Let's see if we can pick her up leaving her home around that time.'

'Who are you talking about?' Anderson stopped mid dip of his biscuit in his tea.

'Sorry, Mrs Marshall,' Crane said. 'She's our only suspect, let's see if we can find her car leaving the garrison, or at least approaching the industrial estate on the night of April's murder.'

'I'll get someone on it,' said Anderson.

'No, it's okay, I don't mind doing a stint. Just point me in the right direction.'

'Fine, come on then. Farnborough have given us direct access to their files, apparently they're stored on the Cloud, wherever that may be and we've a couple of computers set up out here.'

Crane and Anderson walked into the general CID office. Crane looked around an operation that was so much bigger than his own in Provost Barracks. But then it was to be expected. Here was a murder team, hunting a serial killer who had just claimed his or her third victim. Boards were up in strategic places around the room. Some dealt with the post mortems, some the forensic evidence. Others had photos from CCTV and the obvious one of the crime scenes. In one corner of the room was the Office Manager, doling out tasks to his team of civilian employees who were responsible for updating the HOLMES computer system with every piece of information, witness statement or forensic evidence they had. Others were responsible for analysing that information, searching for threads, similarities or variances.

The Senior Investigating Officer, a Chief Superintendent, was just finishing up the morning briefing and with noisy scrapes of chairs teams of detectives stood up, gathered their things and headed for the door.

'You're not involved in that all?' Crane asked, wondering why Anderson wasn't at the briefing.

'Already got my orders for the day, Crane.'

'Which are?'

'Why to keep you in check, of course.'

With Anderson laughing and Crane grumbling, they made their way to a small screened off area where there were two computer monitors, complete with police officers sat in front of them. Crane was inordinately glad to see operators in place. He hadn't too much faith in Anderson's computer skills. His friend was a dinosaur when it came to technology.

He let Anderson brief the two operators and one quickly found the dark hatchback with a foreign number plate on, leaving the Garrison at Hospital Hill.

'Bingo,' said Anderson. 'There she is, now let's follow her...'

A while later, Anderson and Crane took a break for a well-earned cuppa and Crane wanted to go and have a cigarette. Pacing around outside the building, Anderson grumbling something about breathing in secondary smoke and diesel fumes, Crane savoured the welcome nicotine hit and then said, 'Okay so we have her in the vicinity for the latest victim. But now we need to go back and see if we can trace her being around for the other two. We've already got a similar looking woman near Lindsay's murder, but we need to definitively identify her car and track it as far as we can through the cameras for all three murders.' Crane took a deep drag on his cigarette. 'We're closing in Derek,' he said, smoke billowing from his mouth. 'But I've got to be sure before I pull her in. She is the Colonel's wife for God's sake.'

'It might take a few days to trawl through the whole lot,' Anderson warned.

'I don't care. Put more men on it if you can get authority. We've got to trace her from the nearest CCTV camera to her house, through the town and up to the industrial estate. For all three murders.'

'Okay, but you'll have to help. You know the garrison like the back of your hand. There must be so many entrances and exits that she could use if she's varying her route, which is what I'd do. Your knowledge could really help.'

'No worries,' Crane nodded his agreement. 'Draper says I've got to be bloody sure before I go anywhere near her, so to me that gives me carte blanche for staying here if needs be.'

Fifty Five

Driving home from work that evening, Peter was wondering what was going on. He'd heard on the radio news that there had been another victim. Another dead girl. April. April of the warmest, softest lips he'd ever kissed or felt on his body. April with her whole life before her. Why had three of his women been killed? They were girls. People. Human beings. Nice girls who never did any harm. Girls who were only trying to make their way in the world and bring a little comfort and excitement to men along the way. They didn't even charge very much.

His hands were sweating, slick on the steering wheel and he turned on the air conditioning to try and cool himself down. His face was burning and his heart rate galloping. Not even the softness of the leather or the warmth of the walnut dashboard of his car could calm him down. For now he was angry. Angry at the waste of life. Angry that someone could do something so barbaric, killing three girls with shards of glass. Angry that his girls, his guilty secrets, were being killed for no reason that he could think of.

By the time he arrived home he had forced himself

to regain some semblance of control. He knew he couldn't lose his cool. Couldn't give himself away. No one must know. He had to reign in his temper and emotions and pretend like nothing was happening. He climbed out of the car, glad of the cool wind on his face. The trees were bending under the pressure of it, the leaves shivering and shaking. He tried to listen to their message. But they offered him no comfort.

Walking into the house, it was bright and welcoming. It should have been an oasis of calm for him, but Louise couldn't offer the succour he needed. As he walked into the sitting room, the television was showing the local news. Louise was sat in an armchair, leaning forwards, glued to the screen. He wasn't even sure she'd heard him come in.

He turned his attention to the television. A picture of a local policeman filled the picture.

'We are calling on the public for assistance. For anyone who knew the three girls to come forward. All information will be treated in total confidence.'

'What information are you hoping for, DI Anderson?' the news presenter asked the policeman. She was an immaculately groomed woman, making the man sat next to her look like the scarecrow from The Wizard of Oz by comparison.

'We are trying to piece together their last days. Who did they see? Who did they go with? Who knew them? Where did they go?'

'So you want their friends to come forward?'

'Friends, clients, pimps, anyone.' Anderson turned away from the presenter and looked straight into the camera. 'I don't care who you are,' he said. 'This is not about prosecuting those who are involved in the sex trade. This is about finding the cold blooded killer who seems to be preying on working girls.'

At Anderson's words, Peter nearly fainted. His head begun to swim, he could no longer hear the television and he grabbed the back of the settee to steady himself. He couldn't come forward as one of the girl's clients, he just couldn't. And anyway he didn't have any evidence. He didn't know anything. But then he began to wonder once again why three of his girls were dead. The only three he'd gone with, actually. Could all this have any bearing on him? Did anyone know? Should he suspect any of the lads at work? Anyone at home? But then he dismissed the thought of the killer being Louise as total nonsense. They'd been together for 20 years for God's sake. He knew her inside out.

Then, unable to watch the news item any longer, he tore his eyes from the television screen and his gaze lit upon Louise. She was sitting slightly forward in her chair, hands in her lap, mouth slightly open, completely engrossed in the news item. He watched as her tongue licked her lips. She was transfixed. Her eyes were gleaming. When her mouth closed and the sides lifted in a self-satisfied smile Peter had to clamp his mouth shut, grinding his teeth together, to stop the accusation that was building inside him, exploding from his mouth. He chastised himself. Told himself to stop being so stupid. His wife couldn't be the killer. That was the most idiotic idea he'd ever had. He realised how close he'd come to making a bloody fool of himself. Instead of flinging accusations at her, he cleared his throat to catch Louise's attention.

Fifty Six

That evening, Crane arrived home and dumping his stuff in the hallway, he rubbed at his tired eyes. He didn't know how people worked at a computer monitor all day, every day. His eyes were rimmed red and he couldn't seem to shake the blurred vision, no matter how hard he rubbed or blinked.

It was already late and his son was sleeping peacefully in his cot. Crane tip toed into the room and took a moment to look at the sleeping child. Tina and Daniel were really the only ones who ever broke through the hardened shell of his emotions. He was so used to boxing off his feelings, refusing to let himself be affected no matter how awful the crime or the incident, that at work he had become almost an automaton. A self-operating machine. Years ago in school he'd learned of Talon from Greek Mythology. A giant man of bronze who protected Europa in Crete from pirates and invaders. He'd circled the island's shores three times daily. That's who Crane identified with now. He felt himself to be a protector. A man who kept the garrison safe from outside horrors, or from the evil within. There were thousands of inhabitants of

Aldershot Garrison, soldiers and their families, whom he had sworn to protect and serve.

Tina was already in bed, reading by a small light clipped to her bedside table. She smiled as he walked in, but the best he could do was smile in return, take off his clothes and fall into bed beside her. He was asleep in moments. If she spoke to him, he didn't hear her.

It was the following morning, over breakfast, before they had a chance to chat. Crane was taking his turn feeding Daniel breakfast, more of which was ending up on the floor or on his bib, than in his mouth. As she brought over a cup of tea, Tina told Crane she'd seen the Colonel's wife yesterday at the Playgroup.

'Oh, yes?' He was immediately interested. 'Did you get a chance to speak to her?'

'Yes, we chatted for a few minutes,' Tina said and took away Daniel's cereal bowl, before grabbing a cloth to clean up the mess he'd made.

'What did you talk about?'

'Oh, I told her about your latest investigation.'

Crane stopped with his mug of tea half way to his mouth. 'Tina! You know you're not supposed to do that. Jesus! What did you tell her?' He put the mug down before he spilled tea all over his clean suit.

Tina looked crestfallen. 'I told her about you finding the glove covered in blood and the really exciting bit of a speck of blood inside it. If you remember you phoned me yesterday morning gabbling about it.'

Crane closed his eyes to take a moment to think. He didn't want to have a go at Tina. Then something occurred to him. It may have been a good thing, his wife's indiscretion. It all depended on the answer to his next question. He opened his eyes, looked at her and asked, 'What did she say?'

'Well, she went a bit white and looked like she was about to faint. I had to go and get her a glass of water. Sorry, Tom, did I do something wrong?'

'Wrong? Tina my love you are wonderful!'

'Why? Tom?' she called.

But Crane was already leaving the house, slamming the door closed behind him.

Fifty Seven

Louise knew she was in trouble. She'd been panicking since she'd talked to Tina yesterday afternoon, when Crane's wife had gleefully told her all about the glove and the blood. Not realising what she was saying and who she was telling. But this was the first time Louise had been alone since then. For once she and Peter had arrived home more or less at the same time yesterday and it was one of the rare nights when he hadn't gone out, but stayed in. No doubt he was mourning the death of his latest favourite prostitute.

But now that she was alone, she could consider her options. It seemed the police weren't far away from arresting her. Once they analysed the blood and realised it was April's on the outside of the glove and Louise's on the inside, the game would be up. She fingered the small cut on the side of her index finger. She'd hurt herself washing up a sharp knife. The cut had scabbed over, but the scab kept getting caught at the end, causing the wound underneath to bleed again. That must have been what had happened. It was the only reason she could think of for blood having been found inside the leather glove. Louise had no idea how long analysis of the blood would take. No idea when they would come for her.

What should she do? Stay? Go? Flee Aldershot, the county or even the country? But she realised that she had very little resources. She had her car and access to money. Even though it was the beginning of the month and she had the housekeeping money in her account, she knew it wouldn't be enough. It would get her somewhere, but not allow for any living costs. And she didn't know what to do about work. She'd never worked a day in her life.

Should she come clean? Tell Peter? Tell the police? As she paced the house she kept getting glimpses of herself in the mirrors. In them she looked the same. Auburn curls, pale complexion, green eyes. She almost expected the mirrors to reflect what was really inside her, for surely she had turned into a monster. She was someone who had killed three women. Willingly. What did that make her? She imagined a deranged harlot, or a shrivelled up hag lurking inside of her, for surely she was an evil witch. In truth what she was, was a cold blooded murderer.

Then she remembered that what she had done made her a good wife, in fact the perfect wife. Peter couldn't have asked for someone better, she realised. For Louise had looked out for him throughout his army career. Been there at his side. At his elbow. Devoting herself to him, as he devoted himself to the army. They had both been working toward the same end. For all that mattered was Peter's career.

And now it seemed that career was in jeopardy. But it wasn't Louise's fault. It was Peters. She had only tried to clean up the mess that he'd made of his personal life. The mess that threatened his career. No, he'd started this particular ball rolling. He was the one ultimately responsible for getting his whores killed.

But that still didn't answer the question of what to do. So she turned to the only person Louise was confident would have the answer. Matilda. She must get out the book and see how it was to end.

Fifty Eight

And so I come to the last victim. He came to me last night, as I thought he would. I was getting ready for bed when I heard his footsteps on the stairs. The slow steady tread that filled my heart with fear. I saw the door knob turn slowly and with each turn ice flooded through my veins. I would not, could not, endure any more from this man. The door creaked as it opened and there he was. He stood looking at me, one hand still on the handle. Then he stepped through the door and closed it behind him. He turned the key in the lock, put it in his pocket and came towards me. I was mesmerised. All I could do was to stand there, stock still, terror in my heart, yet unable to move. Then he lunged. Quick as a flash he grabbed me and flung me on the bed, climbing up on top of me. I tried to tell him no. Begged him not to hurt me, but he clamped his hand over my mouth to stop my screams. Roughly he pulled up my clothes, ripped my underwear and raped me.

That was what it was. Rape. There was no love involved. No kisses. No whispers of affection. No soft caress. Just raw animal need, which he sought to sate as he thrust into me. When he'd finished, he rolled onto his back, gasping for breath. I was once more discarded. That's when I reached down and retrieved the shard of glass that I had hidden under the bed.

This time it was I above him. He opened his eyes. Saw me

there. His mouth twisted in a grin and he said, 'Oh, you want more then, do you?'

'No,' I replied. 'I don't want you ever again. There is to be no more sex. No more rape. Not ever.'

Then I brought down my shard of glass as hard as I could and pierced the heart of my husband. I looked down on him as though from a great height. I could see his face which still registered the shock of my treachery. His eyes were wide open and his mouth gaping, as though he were gasping for the air that would never again fill his lungs.

For a moment I felt the most incredible jolt of fear. This time I had gone too far. I had killed my own husband in our home, in our bed. Surely there was no way back from that. But then the voice of the house spoke. It pierced my fear, allowing it to evaporate, like air being released from a balloon. The house told me not to worry. Told me that everything would be alright. That I would never have to leave this place. No one could make me.

I could stay within these walls forever.

Safe. Forever.

Warm. Forever.

Loved. Forever.

The house told me to finish the book, wrap it in the headscarf and leave it where the next woman who needed protection from the cruelties of men would find it. Then she, you, would be able to join me. So that's what I have done.

I will now return to my husband and take my own final journey.

I will become one with the house.

Where I will be waiting, for you.

Fifty Nine

After leaving Tina, Crane had gone straight to Aldershot Police Station, where he told Anderson about Mrs Marshall's reaction to Tina, when they had spoken at the Playgroup yesterday.

'Well, that's all very interesting,' said Anderson. 'But the problem remains that we don't have the Colonel's wife's DNA on file. We've nothing to match the blood in the glove with.'

'Is the CCTV evidence enough to question her? After all our hard work yesterday, we've found her car travelling in the direction of the industrial estate at the approximate time of each murder. And back again afterwards. Is it enough to arrest her?' Crane asked.

Crane knew that Draper was blanching at the thought of arresting the Colonel's wife. So was Crane privately. It was something he'd wrestled with on his car journey over to the police station. His desire to protect the army versus his desire to put away a cold blooded killer. But he'd made that choice before. Made the decision to blow a conspiracy wide open. He'd publically outed those in the army who years ago had spirited a killer out of Aldershot as he was needed on the front line. Crane hadn't let them get away with it, despite their rank, despite the silence, despite the cordon of lies they'd created.

And so Crane knew he had no alternative but to pursue the investigation. But Anderson was quick to sense Crane's reluctance.

'This is no time for you to pull the bloody army will investigate themselves bollocks, Crane,' Anderson said. 'You know the score. You can't be part of a conspiracy, or at the very least be seen to be a part of a conspiracy. Murder is a high profile crime. It's just not a military police matter. It's a civilian police matter.'

'It's alright, Derek. I won't be part of a conspiracy. I know that and you know that, but I'm still going to have to tread pretty bloody carefully. We need to try and get as solid a case as possible against Mrs Marshall before we proceed.

'And how will you lot feel if another girl is murdered in the meantime, while you're building a solid case?'

'I know, Derek, there's no need to rub it in. But we still haven't got a real motive.'

'I thought we were going with the fact that it seems the Colonel is using prostitutes. We found his car driving towards the red light district, remember?'

'Is that a good enough reason for Mrs Marshall to kill the girls?'

'We both know people have killed for less,' said Anderson.

Crane had to nod his agreement. 'I know. Right, then, what happens now?'

'Now we have a coffee and cake before we start processing and collating all the paperwork we need for a judge to agree to give us a search warrant.'

By early evening everyone was exhausted, the paperwork for the three murders had been processed and search warrant applications completed and submitted to a judge. They were requesting to search the Colonel's house and his wife's car. Two detectives had gone to Judge Howard's house. They were just waiting for His Honour's decision. Crane was once again in a car park, smoking a cigarette, thinking for the nth time that it really was about time he gave up smoking. But it always seemed there was another crime to stretch his intellect and his nerves and cigarettes were his automatic crutch for getting him through the stresses of the job. His introspection and his cigarette break were interrupted by Anderson appearing at the door.

'Crane?'

'It's a go. His Honour Judge Howard has agreed with us and given us a green light for the searches.'

Crane ground his butt underfoot. 'When do we execute the warrants?'

'The Senior Investigating Officer has said 7 o'clock tomorrow morning. There is nothing more we can do now, so go home and get some rest. Be back here by 6am.'

Crane nodded and walked to his car, hands stuffed into his overcoat. His thoughts as deep as the pockets his hands were in. Crane had cracked some strange cases before, but never one with a Colonel's wife at the centre of it. It made him feel uncomfortable. But he hardened his resolve. He was convinced of Louise Marshall's guilt. He just needed the evidence to prove it.

Sixty

Now that the adrenaline caused by waiting on the warrants had gone, drained away with his anxiety, Crane was knackered. Last night Tina was up when he'd returned home, but not tonight. The house was in darkness and only the outside light above the front door was on.

Making his way quietly into the kitchen, Crane clicked on the kettle then went to check on Daniel and Tina while the water was boiling. Returning downstairs, Crane grabbed a mug and tea bag and stared out of the window while he waited for the kettle to boil. He was absolutely shattered, but no one had told his brain, which was still full of thoughts careering around his head like ping pong balls. Too and fro his thoughts went. He was glad that they were at last making a move, yet worried about the fall out and the disturbing vibes this could have throughout the garrison. It would be open season for the press and television. He'd have to warn Staff Sgt Jones, for if the interest got too bad, they might have to put barriers up on some of the entrances to the garrison.

As he made his cup of tea, he welcomed being back

at home. He had to admit to himself how much he missed his family, when an investigation got as manic as this one had. But he and Tina knew he had a mission in life and it was one he couldn't ignore. They had talked in the past about him leaving the army, giving up the military police. But the role defined him. The army defined him. He could no more make it in civvy street than survive as a fish out of water. And if he was honest he didn't want to try. The only other career he'd contemplate was joining the police force. Anderson had mentioned it once or twice. If Crane or Tina got fed up of the nomadic life, the all-encompassing world that was the British Army, he should consider it. But Crane knew from working with Anderson that joining the police wouldn't solve any of the problems brought on by 12 or 18 hour days. It would only push them from the military over to the police.

So for the time being at least Crane was a member of the armed forces. Proud of the tradition, the men, the honour. It had been his way of life for so long that it fit like a favourite old jumper. Stretched and a bit baggy in places, but warm, comfortable and familiar. Draining his mug of tea, he placed it in the sink, set the alarm on his mobile phone for 5 am and went to join his wife in bed.

Sixty One

The mobile phone next to Crane's bed rang. He fumbled for it, thinking it was his alarm waking him up, but then he realised it was an incoming call and eventually he managed to answer it and held the phone to his ear.

'Sgt Major?' a voice asked.

'Yes,' he mumbled his mouth and mind still full of sleep. He prised open his eyes and stared with horror at the bedside clock. 02:00hours. He'd only slept for two hours.

'I wonder could you come round to the house please?' the voice continued.

Crane struggled against the last vestiges of the dream he'd been having before he was rudely awoken, that was still clogging his brain. He thought he recognised the voice as that of the Colonel's wife. But that couldn't be? Surely not?

'Mrs Marshall, is that you, ma'am?' he asked.

'Yes, Crane. Could you come please?'

'Now, ma'am?'

'Yes. Oh and you might want to bring the police with you.'

The line went dead. He looked at the handset. What the hell was going on? Perhaps she or her husband had got wind of the search warrants, were aware that the net was closing in on Mrs Marshall. But he couldn't see how that had happened. And why was she ringing at two o'clock in the morning? Anyway he had no other option but to comply with her wishes. He got out of bed and fumbled for his dressing gown. He'd go downstairs and ring Draper and Anderson, so as not to wake Tina. But the phone call had already done that.

'Tom? Is everything alright?' Tina raised a sleepy head from where she had been buried under the duvet.

'Yes, love,' Crane smiled in the dark. 'I've got to go out for a while.'

'But you've only just got in.' Tina struggled against the thick bedding and sat up.

'Well, it certainly feels like that at any rate.'

'What's going on?'

'You know, love, I haven't got a bloody clue,' and Crane quickly told her that he was off to the Colonel's house.

'At this time of night?'

'At this time of night,' he agreed.

'I think you're all stark staring mad,' she said and dived under the covers again.

Crane had to totally agree with that sentiment as he ran down the stairs to ring Derek and Draper.

The three men met outside the Colonel's house. The three musketeers, Crane thought glibly. Crane himself, short and stocky, dark hair and short clipped beard. Anderson even more crumpled that usual, sporting a five o'clock shadow, his grey wispy hair ruffled. Draper was the only smart one among them. But, of course, he'd not been involved in the painstaking work of the past few days. He was dressed in uniform, his salt and pepper hair groomed to perfection.

They had parked their cars outside the gates of the Colonel's house and walked through them together. As they walked, their feet crunched on the gravel, an alien sound at that time of night that echoed through the grounds. They reached the house and paused before it. All was quiet. A light breeze ruffled the trees that seemed to be whispering amongst themselves. Did they know Mrs Marshall's secrets? Was that what they were trying to tell Crane? Were they warning him? He pushed aside such foolish thoughts, but was still very much aware that the house and grounds had an air of mystery about them. At least that was the best description he could come up with. He didn't know what it was, but there was definitely something about that house. It was unlike any other army house he'd known. Very large, very grand, very old and a bit of a throwback. As Aldershot Garrison was in the middle of a regeneration programme, building new single men's quarters and married quarters that resembled modern housing estates rather than army barracks, the Colonel's house looked even more incongruous.

'I'll go in as she asked for me,' he said and the other two nodded their agreement.

He walked towards the door put his hand up to the bell and hesitated. He turned the door handle instead, which opened under his hand.

He called out, 'Mrs Marshall? Sir? Is there anyone there?'

That last phrase left Crane feeling a bit foolish, as though he were in some sort of ghost story, or playing with an Ouija board. There was no answer. The downstairs of the house was in darkness, but upstairs there was a light on, its beam filtering down through the impressive staircase. Turning and shrugging at the others, Crane walked up the stairs.

Mrs Marshall must have heard his footsteps, for as he reached the landing he heard her call, 'In here, Sgt Major,' and he followed her voice into a bedroom.

He walked into the room, not really knowing what to expect. Not knowing why the Colonel's wife had called him to her house. What he saw chilled him, like no other crime scene had done before. To find the Colonel dead in his own bed, with a shard of glass sticking out of his chest, was so far from what he'd expected, it stopped him dead in his tracks. He'd imagined they'd caught a burglar, or a young soldier pissing about high on drugs or alcohol, but not this. Never this unexpected tableau of murder and madness, the Colonel dead in his bed with his wife looking calmly on.

Mrs Marshall was sitting by the bed in a small armchair and appeared to be reading some sort of scrap book. She looked up at him. Crane was afraid he was losing his mind. He didn't trust his eyes anymore. Thought that they were lying to him. He looked again from the dead Colonel to his very much alive wife. As he looked more closely at her, he could see she had blood on her hands and splashes of it on her face. Her hair was not just out of place, but in wild ringlets around her head and her lipstick was smudged, making her lips look larger than normal. He thought she looked like she was done up in some sort of Halloween costume, particularly with those piercing green eyes of hers.

She said, 'Perfect timing, Crane, I've just finished.'

Finished what he wondered. Finished reading? Finished killing her husband? As far as Crane was concerned his timing hadn't been perfect, for he was too late. Too late to save the Colonel. It was Crane's job to find killers and bring them to justice and he'd let Peter Marshall down. The Colonel's own wife must have been killing the prostitutes, just as Crane had always suspected, and it seemed her final victim was not another girl, but her husband.

Mrs Marshall followed Crane's gaze as he once more looked at Peter Marshall's dead body. 'Ah yes,' she said, 'that was me. You'll find the other shards of glass from the broken mirror in a box down in the cellar. The ones I haven't used that is.'

Other shards? What the hell was she talking about? Is that what she'd used to kill the prostitutes? Shards of glass from her broken mirror? Yes, that made some sort of sense, he supposed.

'Ma'am,' he said. 'What's happened? Have you? Did you…' For once, Crane was unable to finish his sentence.

Louise Marshall smiled at him, as though indulging a small child. 'You'll find the answers you seek in here,' she said, and handed him the scrap book.

Crane took it after shaking out a handkerchief to hold it with. He looked at the cover. Two words were embossed on it.

Louise Marshall.

'Crane?' he heard the voice of Captain Draper, calling from the doorway. As he turned to his boss and DI Anderson, Crane took his eyes off Louise Marshall.

Sixty Two

Louise afforded herself a small smile, a delicious one. She'd seen Crane's reaction, noted his incredulity. She'd never thought she would be able to out-fox the seasoned investigator. But her final swan song had done just that. She'd been the one step ahead of him that she'd needed to be. So that she could go out on her terms. Not his and not the police's.

Once she'd realised he was on to her, thanks to his gossiping wife, she'd had to act fast. She'd greedily drunk in the final chapter of Matilda's book. How foolish she'd been not to see the way herself, she'd realised. It all made perfect sense now. How clever her friend Matilda was. How clever the house, the house that Louise had come to love as much as Matilda had. In fact she loved it as much as she loved Matilda. For Matilda had been her only friend, her confidant. The one person who'd provided an anchor in the sea of her husband's treachery, when he'd had the temerity to threaten his career, their life together and their home. The home that Louise couldn't bear to leave.

She watched as Crane looked helplessly at the two men with him. Indicating the red leather bound book in his hand. Clearly wondering what it was. The one Louise thought was the policeman, the crumpled one who resembled Columbo, just stared at her with flat eyes. She guessed he'd seen some awful things before. Perhaps this was just one more for him. The soldier in uniform, however, wasn't taking it as well. He was holding onto the door frame, looking decidedly pale under that swarthy tan a lot of soldiers had, the colouring that came from spending so much time outdoors.

Then before any of the men could react, while they were still looking at the book Crane held in his hands, Louise lifted a final shard of glass to her throat and with a smile on her face and in her eyes, went to join her friend Matilda.

Sixty Three

Pru Jenkins looked around the sitting room of their new home. She was surrounded by boxes and wondered when she'd ever get straight. At that moment it seemed like a daunting task and instead of diving into another box, she felt the need to stop and have a cup of tea. Walking from the sitting room into the hallway that took her breath away every time she walked through it, she thought how lucky they were to have found this amazing house, and at such an amazing price. If it hadn't been such a bargain, they'd never have been able to afford such a beautiful home. She'd been resigned to buying a modern three bedroomed box when her husband Ken had told her they were relocating from Newcastle to the south of England, as he'd secured the promotion he wanted and deserved.

When she found the Victorian detached house on the outskirts of Aldershot, within their price range, she couldn't wait to view it. She hoped it would live up to her expectations and it had in every way. It was perfect, just the kind of house befitting a company director.

Walking into the huge kitchen at the end of the hall Pru wondered why the army had decided to sell the house. To her it was perfect for some sort of high ranking officer. She'd never managed to get a straight answer from the local estate agent. But hey, why worry, for their loss was her gain. While the kettle was boiling she decided to put some of the now empty boxes in the cellar. She ripped the brown tape off the cardboard flaps and flattened the boxes, so they'd be easier to carry.

Struggling down the steps, she dumped the boxes at the back of the cellar. Out of sight, out of mind, she thought. As she turned to go back to the stairs, she saw something out of the corner of her eye. Stopping, she saw it was an old chest of some sort that she'd not noticed before. Walking over to it, she knelt down and ran her hand over the brittle leather and saw the clasp was undone. Opening the lid, she spied something white nestled in the bottom. Reaching in, she lifted out a white scarf that appeared to be covering something rectangular and heavy. Peeling off the scarf, she saw it was a red leather bound book of some kind with two words embossed on the cover.

Matilda Underwood.

Past Judgment
Author Note

Her Majesty's Young Offenders Institute (HMYOI) in Reading is no longer a working institute. However, the building is still there and plans are being considered by Reading Council to turn it into a hotel and leisure complex.

The prison has a long and rich history and its most notable prisoner was Oscar Wilde, who wrote the Ballad of Reading Goal, based on his incarceration there.

I worked as a teacher in the Education Department at Reading HMYOI, teaching a range of subjects including English, Maths, Computer Skills, Art and, rather badly, Cookery. I loved my time at Reading and also at other nearby prisons, where I did supply teaching. My family has experience in prison education. My father was Deputy Chief Education Officer for Prisons and Borstals in England and Wales in the 1970's and 1980's and my mother taught at Reading Prison and Broadmoor. Both had the dubious pleasure of meeting some of Britain's most notorious prisoners.

Whilst the Judgment series may draw on our experiences from time to time, all characters and events are fictitious. Although I try and be true to policies and procedures, this is a work of fiction. Therefore, all mistakes are my own.

About Past Judgment

The past has a way of catching up with you....

At least it does for Emma Harrison, newly appointed assistant governor for inmate welfare at Reading Young Offender's Institute and for Leroy Carter, a prisoner who has been convicted of murder. When the prison van taking Leroy to Dartmoor crashes and he escapes, he's hell-bent on proving his innocence.

Leroy and the original detectives on his case, have to face the past head on. But so does Emma, when a fellow passenger from the train hijack three years earlier walks back into her life.

Can Leroy prove his innocence? And has Emma exorcised the ghosts from her past?

1
Present day...

The prison transport vehicle Leroy was expected to climb into loomed into view. It was very large and very white and would carry him away from Reading Young Offenders Institute. From the security of all things known. His well practiced and comfortable routine. His cell mate, John. His courses in the Education Block. And, of course, Emma. Or rather Miss Harrison. He shrank back. Fearful. Unwilling to get into the claustrophobic cell he would be locked in. He turned slightly as if to run away, but the prison escort officer he was handcuffed to wasn't having any of it.

"Come on, lad. Leroy isn't it? In you go, it's not that bad when you get in there."

Leroy had to disagree with that one and wondered if the escort had ever had to travel in one of those 'cells' for any length of time.

"But..."

"No buts, in you go," and Leroy took one last deep breath of fresh air before he and his three travelling companions were pushed and pulled into the vehicle as though they were no more than cattle being herded into a milking shed or an abattoir. As Leroy climbed the two steps into the transport, he was told to stop opposite the second cubicle on his left. When he was told to get in it, Leroy looked at the escort then at the cubicle and wondered how the hell he was supposed to do that. There was very little room in the narrow space to even turn around. Especially for someone as tall and gangly as he was. Standing at over six foot, but without the bulk and muscle to make him intimidating, Leroy had taken to stooping over slightly. A posture that screamed leave me alone, I'm trying to make myself small so as not to be noticed.

"Back in, then I'll close the door and you can hold out your hands through the space in the bars," the exasperated officer told him. "Then I'll un-cuff you and you can turn and sit down."

Leroy managed to do as he was told as the door was banged shut. Then locked. Breathing deeply to try and stop the rush of claustrophobia from his brain flooding through his body, he looked out of the window. Glad for the small glimpse of the world outside. Focusing on the window, he tried to block out the noises of the back door being slammed and locked and then the cab doors being opened and closed. As the rumble of the diesel engine started its soundtrack to their journey, the van left Reading HMYOI, rumbling along the urban roads on its way to the motorway.

As they started their creaky, bumpy journey, Leroy's fellow prisoners made their feelings known. At the top of their voices. From abuse hurled at the escort officers and each other, to sexual references tossed in the direction of any woman unlucky enough to be passing by. They seemed to have an opinion on everything and everyone. Leroy added an extra layer on top of his claustrophobia. Fear. He was straight out scared of his fellow travellers. He hoped this noise and abuse wasn't a sign of things to come at Dartmoor Prison. So far the whole experience wasn't a good start to his new life in a new prison. He shrunk away from the noise, trying to blot it out, pushing back into the seat and turning slightly, trying to keep his back to the other prisoners.

Once on the motorway, the gentle rumble of tyres on asphalt calmed Leroy and he was able to relax a little and inspect his surroundings. Not that it took very long. He was sat on a grey plastic seat in a space smaller than an old fashioned telephone box. But a Dr Who Tardis this wasn't. The space wasn't larger inside than it seemed on the outside. White plastic was everywhere, gouged with irreverent messages from previous occupants. There was nothing to read, nothing to occupy his mind and he sunk into a daze. He became drowsy and must have dozed off, for he was woken by a dramatic clap of thunder.

The view outside his aircraft-type window was obscured by dark heavy clouds. They looked full of the rain they seemed determined to dump on the road. He watched with mounting fascination as the big fat heavy rain drops began to fall. One, two, four, eight, sixteen... until they fell so fast Leroy couldn't count them anymore. The drops fell faster and harder, bouncing ankle high off the ground, their rapid tattoo drilling into his brain. A tattoo that became louder as the raindrops turned into hailstones, some as large as golf balls. They carpeted the road, turning it into a white, icy, highway to hell.

The van, unable to find purchase on the road, began to veer first one way and then the other and Leroy, with nothing to hold onto, put his arms out and placed his hands palm up on each wall. Wet with sweat, they simply slid off the plastic. As the van swerved, Leroy went with it, unable to do anything but ride the storm. He heard tyres squeal as the van slewed sideways. With a bang, the van hit an unseen object and fell over, sliding along the road as though it were still on its wheels, not on its side. Leroy was thrown out of his seat and ended up lying, face down on the side wall that had suddenly become the floor.

After several seconds of screeching metal grinding against the road and Leroy feeling like he was on fairground ride, the transport ground to a halt. For a moment all was still. The kind of pregnant pause found inside the eye of a tornado. The brief period of calm, before the world descended into chaos once again. The other prisoners all began shouting at once. Cursing the weather, the officers and the van. But underneath their yells Leroy could hear something else. He tuned out the yelling from his fellow prisoners as best he could, concentrating on the underlying sound. He recognised it as water. Water that was gushing and gurgling. That's when Leroy realised the van must have fallen into a river. His fears were confirmed when he felt his trousers getting wet. Water was permeating the prison van, seeking out and finding the smallest of gaps. Unchecked. Leroy and his fellow prisoners couldn't get away. The cubicles, so small and narrow, meant they were unable to stand. The doors were locked so they were unable to escape. There was no sign of the escorts. And the water was rising.

You can purchase Past Judgment at Amazon.

Meet the Author

I do hope you've enjoyed Glass Cutter. If so, perhaps you would be kind enough to post a review on Amazon. Reviews really do make all the difference to authors and it is great to get feedback from you, the reader.

If this is the first of my novels you've read, you may be interested in the other Sgt Major Crane books, following Tom Crane and DI Anderson as they take on the worst crimes committed in and around Aldershot Garrison. At the time of writing there are seven Sgt Major Crane crime thrillers. In order, they are: Steps to Heaven, 40 Days 40 Nights, Honour Bound, Cordon of Lies, Regenerate, Hijack and this one, Glass Cutter.

Past Judgment is the first in a new series. It is a spin-off from the Sgt Major Crane novels and features Emma Harrison from Hijack and Sgt Billy Williams of the Special Investigations Branch of the Royal Military Police. At the time of writing the second book, Mortal Judgment has just been released. Look out for more adventures from Billy and Emma in the Judgment series in the near future.

All my books are available on Amazon.

You can keep in touch through my website http://www.wendycartmell.webs.com. I'm also on Twitter @wendycartmell.

Printed in Great Britain
by Amazon